W9-CEP-762

Summer
ON THE
SHORT BUS

BETHANY
CRANDELL

RP|TEENS
PHILADELPHIA · LONDON

Hillside Public Library

Copyright © 2014 by Bethany Crandell
All rights reserved under the Pan-American and
International Copyright Conventions

Printed in the United States

*This book may not be reproduced in whole or in part, in any form or by any means, electronic
or mechanical, including photocopying, recording, or by any information storage and retrieval
system now known or hereafter invented, without written permission from the publisher.*

Books published by Running Press are available at special discounts for
bulk purchases in the United States by corporations, institutions, and other
organizations. For more information, please contact the Special Markets
Department at the Perseus Books Group, 2300 Chestnut Street, Suite 200,
Philadelphia, PA 19103, or call (800) 810-4145, ext. 5000, or
e-mail special.markets@perseusbooks.com.

ISBN 978-0-7624-4951-4

Library of Congress Control Number: 2014931178
E-book ISBN 978-0-7624-5198-2

9   8   7   6   5   4   3   2   1
Digit on the right indicates the number of this printing

Designed by Frances J. Soo Ping Chow
Illustrated by T.L. Bonaddio
Edited by Marlo Scrimizzi
Typography: American Pop, Baskerville, Bookeyed Nelson,
Univers, Valencia, Voluta Script, and Zapf Dingbats

Published by Running Press Teens
An Imprint of Running Press Book Publishers
A Member of the Perseus Books Group
2300 Chestnut Street
Philadelphia, PA 19103–4371

Visit us on the web!
www.runningpress.com/kids

To Mom,
Save a place for me

ONE

Less than forty-eight hours ago I was in the comfort of my room, thick in a conversation with my best friend about those red patent Miu Miu ballet flats we saw in the Neiman's catalog, when in full, dickhead parent mode, my dad stormed in and single-handedly destroyed my entire summer.

"Constance Elaine," he said in a deep voice. "I have never been more disappointed with you in my entire life. You should be ashamed of yourself."

We'd had conversations like this before, so I knew there was no reason to get my panties all twisted up. I just responded the same way I always do: I dropped my head slightly and conjured up my best Bambi eyes. "Aw . . . come on, Dad. It wasn't *that* bad."

"Actually, yes!" he said, surprisingly unaffected. "It really *was* that bad."

Looking back, I admit having an impromptu party in the riding stables wasn't the best idea, but I'm seventeen. If I can't screw off a little now, when can I? And who was that stable hand to call *me* out anyway? Doesn't he know my father practically owns that place?

"So what?" I challenged, surprised by his sudden display of

badassedness. "You going to ground me or something?"

He sighed deeply and his face contorted into that sad, wounded puppy look he hasn't worn since the last time I asked about my mom. "Honestly, Cricket . . . I'm not sure what I'm going to do with you."

Well, he might not have known right that minute, but he figured it out pretty fast. The next morning he chewed my ass about the privileged life I lead, going on about how I have no concept of what happens in the real world and how my selfish behavior is getting out of hand. He puffed up like a bullfrog and croaked something about making sure I leave for college next year with a good head on my shoulders and my feet planted firmly on the ground. It was one of those lame, parental speeches that was supposed to motivate me to change my ways, or start journaling my feelings. In the end, all it did was piss me off.

And as if lecturing me until I was ready to ram scissors in my ears wasn't bad enough, he salted the wound by announcing that not only was he confiscating my credit cards until school started, but I would not be flying to Maui with Katie and her family as planned. Instead, I would be spending the rest of my summer acting as a camp counselor to a bunch of tweens who are too lame to know that summer camp stopped being cool when you were seven. Surely this was some sort of sick joke.

TWO

We've been driving nearly two hours and I'm beginning to suspect that my dad wasn't kidding after all. The landscape outside the town car has steadily evolved from the buildings, shops, and urban life that are familiar sights in downtown Chicago, to this . . . I don't even know what you'd call it. There's just a crapload of trees and more Buicks than a car dealership.

I pull out my iPhone for the fourteenth time, hoping maybe this will be the minute Katie decides to turn her phone on, when I see Sean's dark eyes glance at me through the rearview mirror.

"This is going to be a good thing for you, Constance."

"Don't call me that. And mind your own business!" I glare back at him, my phone shoved against my ear. The last thing I need is my dad's personal driver thinking he can offer me any reassurance that this situation isn't as completely jacked up as it is.

"Katie, it's me," I whine into her voice mail. Again. "Pleeeeease call me. I'm dying here."

Through the rearview, I see that Sean's eyes are still steady on me. I turn back to my phone and update my Facebook status. It now reads: WANT TO HANG YOURSELF? COME TO MICHIGAN—

PLENTY OF TREES!

An eternity passes without any response from Katie. I'm seriously considering opening the door and giving myself a road rash tattoo, when Sean has the balls to say, "Your dad thinks this will be a good learning experience for you, *Cricket*. You know, he's doing this because he loves you."

"Oh please! Spare me, Sean. Just because you drive me from point A to point B doesn't mean you know anything about my life. You drive the car! And as for my father doing this because he loves me . . . well, he obviously doesn't love me enough to cancel his trip to Madrid so he can drive me up here himself. So just do me a favor and keep your opinions to yourself, okay?"

"Okay," he says with an ease that makes me want to scream. "I'll keep my opinions to myself. Just remember one thing: I've gotten to know your father pretty well in the fifteen years I've been working for him, and I can tell you without any hesitation that he loves you more than anything in this world—including trips to Spain."

"Noted. Now I'd really like to get through the rest of this painful trip in silence, if you don't mind."

"Nope," he says in that same infuriating tone. "I don't mind one bit."

Seconds later the tinted privacy screen rises between the front and back seats, leaving only my annoyed reflection on the glass in front of me and countless trees on either side of the car.

Kill me now.

A while later we pull off the highway and onto a single-lane road marked with a small green sign that reads: CAMP I CAN, 1 MILE.

Now that we're nearing our godforsaken destination, I recognize that the intense anger I've been feeling for the last two-and-a-half hours has evolved into mind-numbing fear. What if this is a cult where they learn Bible verses and chant around the campfire? Or worse, *God*, what if it's a fat camp?

My stomach starts knotting up as Sean follows the road around several winding bends beneath a canopy of trees and through an arched wooden sign that reads: WELCOME, CAMPERS!

"Somebody shoot me," I grumble, just as Sean drops the privacy glass.

"We're here, Cricket."

"Obviously."

Through the mirror I see that the corners of his eyes are crinkling with amusement. Asshole.

The car slows to a crawl as we make our way through a steel gate and onto the property. Out the side windows the view is nothing but trees and shrubs, though the windshield provides a much different view: a health inspector's wet dream. It's a huge wooden structure with a green tin roof, two windowless front doors, and a rusted-out dinner bell that must have gone down with the *Titanic*. There's a hillbilly porch that wraps around the entire building, a collection of steel rocking chairs, and even a pair of oak barrel planters with overgrown geraniums spilling out of them.

How freaking quaint.

"Looks like this is the spot." Sean motions his head to the right, where a handful of people are staring at our car. Each of them is wearing the same T-shirt and overworked smile.

It's definitely a cult.

As the car comes to a halt, the group disappears behind a blanket of dust.

"I don't think you're supposed to just dump me here," I say as Sean pops open the trunk. "My dad will be pissed if you leave me with a bunch of strangers."

"Your father is the one who arranged this, Cricket. I'm sure there's nothing to worry about." Sean climbs out of the car, leaving me unprotected from the nightmare unfolding around me. Tummy reeling, I stare blankly at the seat in front of me. I've never felt so alone in my life.

I look out my window and see a middle-aged woman approaching with a freakishly big grin on her face. Unfortunately, her outdated Ray-Bans make it impossible for me to get a look at her eyes, so I base my initial impression on the rest of her appearance—which is tragic at best. Skinny, knobby-kneed, with flame-red hair pulled back into a tangled ponytail and skin resembling glue. She's quite possibly the least attractive woman I've ever seen. The gleaming white CAMP I CAN T-shirt isn't doing her any favors, either.

Always the professional, Sean greets the ghost-white stranger with a handshake and a manufactured smile. I press the button on my right, cracking the window so I can eavesdrop on their conversation.

"You must be Rainbow. I'm Sean, Mr. Montgomery's personal driver. It's a pleasure to meet you."

Rainbow? Oh hell, no! I am not about to spend my summer with a bunch of tree-hugging green freaks! She probably doesn't even shave her pits.

"Happy to meet you, too," she says, a little too enthusiastically. She cranes her neck to the right, looking past Sean's large frame and into the front passenger window. In a nearly inaudible voice she says, "Carolyn wasn't able to make it?"

Carolyn? How could she possibly know my housekeeper, or think that she'd be along for the ride? Sure Carolyn and I have had our issues over the years, but there's no way she'd be in on this urban kidnapping mission. She was just as upset about it as I was.

I think back to the brief and surprisingly emotional conversation we had earlier this morning.

"Here. You're going to need these," she had said, shoving a pack of my favorite peppermints into my hand.

Ordinarily I'd have been thrilled to receive a bag of my favorite candy, but today they felt like a last meal wrapped up in a sweet, pink package. Accepting them would mean all of this was real.

"Carolyn, *please*. You can't let him do this."

"What am I to do?" she said, shrugging. "He's your father, Constance. I'm just the housekeeper."

Tears started welling behind my eyes and I turned away from her. "I can't believe you're just going to let him ship me off. You don't care at all."

"Oh, stop that, now." As she'd done when I was a child, she raised my chin with her age-spotted hand so I had nowhere to look other than her face. "You know that I love you. I would do something if I could, but there was no way I could convince your father."

"Did you even try?"

She shrugged helplessly as her blue eyes softened around the edges. "Maybe it will be good for you."

Sometimes the remnants of her Eastern European upbringing made understanding her a little difficult. But this morning, her words rang loud and clear. Nobody could do anything to change his mind.

I sink back into my seat and heave a deep breath before I start getting choked up again. Unfortunately, the therapeutic scent of the leather interior is doing nothing for my nerves. If I had eaten any breakfast I have no doubt it would be making a second appearance right about now.

Several painful moments pass before Sean opens my door. The sticky summer heat pours into the car, sending a flush of goose bumps across my skin.

Oh my God. This is actually happening.

"This is Cricket," Sean says. "She's really happy to be here. Aren't you, Cricket?"

I give Sean my famous die-now glare before sliding my Cavalli frames back into place and climbing out of the car.

"Cricket!" the Rainbow woman chirps. She approaches me with her arms spread wide enough to embrace a cow. I reel my head back, offended at the notion. "Oh," she murmurs, her smile retreating to the crannies of her doughy skin while her arms fall limply to her sides. "Well . . . hi. I'm Rainbow Millsap," she says after clearing her throat. "I can't tell you how thrilled we are to have you here this summer. I've been looking forward to . . . *meeting* you for a long time."

"I'm sure."

She casts a skeptical glance in Sean's direction before saying, "Well, I won't send you into information overload your first five minutes, but I want to assure you that we take the special needs of our campers very seriously. And if there's anything I can do to make this transition easier for you, just let me know. I'm sure we'll have you up to speed in no time."

Does a special need include fetching me a syringe full of Valium?

"First, I'd like to introduce you to the staff," she says all too eagerly. "Are you up for that?"

I drop my chin to my chest and peer over my lenses at the five silhouettes behind her. "Yeah, whatever."

Rainbow arches a brow at Sean. From the corner of my eye I see him shrug, as if to say, "Hey lady, she's your problem now."

"Well, all right then," she says, suddenly more businesslike. "Why don't you grab your bag and we'll get this show on the road."

Before I can even ask who to call for bell service, my pink duffel lands directly in front of my flip-flopped feet. "Here you go." Sean smiles down at me with those damn eye creases still firmly set and taunting. "Have fun."

My breath suddenly gets caught up in my chest, making it impossible to breathe. "You're not really going to leave me here, are you?"

"You're in good hands," he says, patting my head like I'm some orphaned puppy. "And this is what your dad wanted. You'll be fine."

I open my mouth to protest the unfairness of this, but it's too late. Sean is already back in the car, and within seconds, he's disappearing down the gravely road while I'm left with a bunch of strangers, abandoned in a cloud of exhaust fumes and dust.

"Ready?" Rainbow asks, suddenly right beside me.

I sidestep away from her. Ready for what exactly? Braiding hemp bracelets by the moonlight? Sacrificing small farm animals?

"As if I have a choice," I say.

Suddenly grateful for her little gift, I find one of the peppermints Carolyn gave me and pop it into my mouth, before tucking the rest into the pocket of my duffel bag.

"As I mentioned before, my name is Rainbow and I'm the director here at Camp I Can. I've been on staff for over fifteen years, and have been director for the past eleven. I'm the only full-time, year-round employee. The rest of the staff is summers only—like you."

Oh God. I'm staff.

"We have three two-week camp sessions every summer with different counselors for each session," she continues. "This team has worked together for the last three years."

With the strap of my bag threatening to rip my shoulder out of its socket, we make our way to the line of identically dressed losers standing behind her.

"This is Colin," she says, stopping in front of an enormous black guy whose knees are about level with my forehead. "Colin is the supervisor for all of the physical activities. We have swimming, archery, hiking—"

"Anything you can think of," he interrupts, offering me his enormous hand and a glimpse of a shockingly big, Crest-whitened grill. "How you doin', Cricket?"

"Okay, I guess."

"Just okay?"

I shrug. As if one word could possibly describe how I'm really feeling.

"Well, I'm sure we'll have you feeling better than *okay* in no time," he says and smiles so wide his face all but disappears.

"Right." I give my hand a quick shake so blood can return to my fingers.

"And this is Fantine," Rainbow says. She stops in front of a girl about my age who has skin the color of iced tea and a mane of curly copper hair that cascades across her toned shoulders. "Fantine supervises our arts and crafts activities, and she's your bunkmate."

Bunkmate?

"Hey, girl." Fantine's voice is soulful, sounding older than her years. It makes me think she could sing songs about being dumped. "I know it's a lot to take in, but you'll get used to it in no time. And don't worry, I hardly snore anymore."

I feel my cheeks warm as I realize Rainbow's not kidding. I actually have to share a room with this girl. Which means I'll probably have to share a bathroom, too. Holy shit . . .

"Next, we have the troublemaker of the operation." The entire group laughs at a joke I don't get, just as Rainbow wraps her arm around a tiny man who could double as the Travelocity gnome if he had the right hat. "This is Sam. Sam is our head chef."

The older man smiles, forcing his beady eyes to disappear into the folds of his cheeks. "I'm a chef. A good chef. Not a cook."

"That's right, Sam," Rainbow agrees with a nod. "You are a *chef*!"

"Hey, Cricket, I'm Pete." A twentysomething guy with strawberry-blond hair and more freckles than Rainbow takes my hand before I can contemplate what's wrong with the little gnome-chef. "I'm in charge of applying Band-Aids," he says.

"Among other things," Rainbow interjects. "Pete's a second-year medical student and a far cry from Band-Aid distributor, though he does do that sometimes. And very well, I might add."

"I do apply a mean Band-Aid," he says, winking at me with one of his startlingly light blue eyes.

"I'll keep that in mind," I say.

"And last, but not least, is Quinn."

My eyes wander to what is sure to be the biggest joker in this poorly dealt hand. But as I take in his tanned body and eyes that are the same color blue as my favorite Slurpee, it's all I can do not to melt into a puddle right here on the ground. "Oh my God," I whisper, suddenly breathless. "You look just like . . ."

"Please don't say it," he says, rolling his eyes. "Please don't."

"Un-uh, Quinn!" Fantine is now at my side, laughing. "She has every right to tell you her opinion. Go ahead, girl. He just *loves* it when people tell him who he looks like."

I raise my glasses for a better look.

"Straight up, Cricket. This is his favorite part of camp," Colin adds from miles above me. "That's why he's blushing. He loves it."

"You guys suck, you know that?" Quinn shakes his head while a grin starts inching its way across his face. "For the record," he says, "I don't play basketball, I never sing in public, and I *definitely* don't dance."

"He's never even seen *High School Musical*," Pete adds, not wanting to be excluded.

"You're just . . . I mean, you're so . . ." Good God! What is wrong with me? "You look just like him!" I finally squeal.

"Wait until you see the campers with him." Rainbow sidles up beside Quinn and traps him beneath one of her long giraffe arms. "Last year it took a couple of days for them to stop calling him Zac and start calling him Quinn. They asked him for his autograph for weeks!"

"Can I pleeeease have an autograph, Mr. Efron?" Fantine says with a snort and drops to her knees in front of him. "Just one autograph?"

The entire group, including Quinn, bursts into laughter.

"It's unbelievable," I say, and realize I'm laughing, too. "But at least you look like a hottie. Can you imagine how much it would suck if you were mistaken for some deformed freak . . . like Quasimodo?"

Rather than the laughter I expect, all I get is an earful of deafening silence. What the hell? I take in the faces of everyone around me—every open jaw and wide eye gaping at me.

"Um . . . right. Okay then, everybody," Rainbow says and drags a hand across her forehead. I'm not sure how it's possible, but she's paler than she was five seconds ago. "Fantine, why don't you give Cricket the five-dollar tour while we finish getting things ready for the arrivals."

"With pleasure," Fantine mumbles. She glances at the rest of the staff before sauntering past me without another word. I look up at Quinn, his face as unreadable as everyone else's, and realize that I've just committed some forbidden camp counselor crime.

"Whatever," I say, and turn to follow Fantine. It's not like I care what a bunch of dorks in matching white T-shirts think about me anyway. Even if one of them does look like a movie star.

THREE

Our first stop on the half-assed tour is the mess hall, aka the needs-to-be-condemned building I saw when we first drove in. All meals are eaten here, which means I can add food poisoning to my growing list of fears. The mess hall is also the location for special activities like movie night and the end-of-summer battle of the bands. It's all so riveting I can hardly stand it.

"The archery range and pool are down that way," Fantine says while nodding toward a paved trail that cuts through a grassy field and disappears behind what looks like an outhouse. "Over here is where the boys sleep." She hesitates in front of a large, A-framed cabin with a BOYS RULE, GIRLS DROOL sign hanging from the door. "Colin and Quinn stay in there, and that's their bathroom." I look up the hill and see a tiny building with a bright orange roof and faded red door. From my vantage point I don't think Colin could fit through it, let alone get comfy enough to take a dump.

"Uh . . . where's our bathroom?"

"On the other side of the hill by our cabin. Come on."

Fantine scurries up the hill with the dexterity of a panther, while I am left to struggle through the sticks in my Marc Jacobs flip-flops with my thousand-pound bag hanging off my shoulder.

"God, Fantine, this is heavy! Can you just wait a second?"

"You don't do much for yourself, do you?"

"What?" I pause to catch my breath and look up to find her standing a few feet above me, her hands on her hips and a smirk on her face. "I'm carrying the bag myself, in case you haven't noticed."

"Right," she says coolly. "That's exactly what I meant. Do you think you can make it another ten feet, or do I need to call for an ambulance?"

"Very funny!" I say before redirecting wisps of blonde hair from my face with a sweaty arm. Fantine sighs and continues up the hill again. I follow along, groaning the entire way.

"This is our place," she says, pointing to yet another ram-shackle building. The sign hanging above the screen door says GIRLS RULE, BOYS DROOL. How original.

"Come on, I'll show you where you can put your stuff."

My tour guide blows through the door as if it were a five star resort, while I'm left slugging my bag up the rickety, wood-rotted steps in the nine-hundred-degree heat.

"You know, you took the hard way." She pops her head through the doorway just as I reach the landing sweat-soaked and completely out of breath. "I think the ramp would've been a much better choice for you."

I glance to my right and see a long, wood-planked ramp that

runs the length of the building all the way to the platform where I stand. Now she tells me.

She props the left of two doors open with her Nike-covered foot, inviting me into the dank space with a cold stare. The moment my foot hits the worn floor my stomach drops.

"You're kidding, right?"

"About what?"

"About this!" I say, motioning to the eyesore around me. "You don't actually sleep in here, do you? It smells like wet socks, and there's no carpet on the floor." I peer down at my dirt-covered feet and nearly burst into tears. My pedicure is totally ruined. "You can't tell me that parents actually *pay* for their children to sleep in accommodations like these."

"Actually, they do. The ones that can afford to, anyway," she says with a look that could make puppies cry. "And for the record, their children love it. Our beds are in here." Sliding a faded yellow curtain from the wall, she reveals a tiny room housing two wood-framed cots, a cracked window no bigger than an economy-fare porthole, and a shelving system made of plywood, cinder blocks, and about two thousand spiderwebs. "You can have the top shelf."

I seriously consider bolting and running for my life, but I can't move. My feet are cemented to the floor and I'm having trouble breathing.

"Why are you even here?"

"What?" I ask, still trying to catch a breath.

"Why are you here?" she asks me again, her dark eyes burrowing into my soul. "It's pretty obvious you don't want to be."

I swallow through a newly formed knot in my throat—I hope she's not violent.

"The way I see it, there are only two kinds of people who show up here at the last minute. There's the last-ditch, need-something-impressive-on-my-college-application people who think they can come here for the summer and skate through without making any real effort. And then there's the stuck-up rich kids who get busted shoplifting and are avoiding their juvy sentence by opting for community service. So tell me, Cricket. Which one are you?"

"Oh my God! Do I look like I belong in juvy?"

She raises a sculpted brow.

"My dad set this whole thing up because he wants me to be more grounded or something," I say, quickly rethinking my initial strategy of telling her to screw off. "Trust me. There are about a thousand other places I'd rather be than here."

"Well, aren't we the lucky ones," she says and takes a slightly less aggressive stance, which does little to pacify my nerves. "All right, here's the deal, Cricket. It goes against my instincts, but I'm willing to assume that you're only acting like a judgmental bitch because this is a new experience for you. I know this isn't your typical summer camp and it takes some getting used to. But what you need to understand is that we love this camp, we love these kids, and we take our jobs seriously. It's a lot more than something

Daddy just arranged to keep us out of trouble. So if you think I'm going to let beach-blanket Barbie with her Fendi bag roll in here and ruin my summer, you got another think coming. You feel me?"

I suddenly feel like I'm playing the lead in a bad ABC Family movie where I'm the pretty rich girl whose parents die and is forced to live with foster parents in the inner city. Their biological daughter hates me because her gangster boyfriend, who's actually smart and misunderstood, likes me more than her, so she challenges me to a dance-off or cheer competition.

"Yeah," I say in a near whisper, "I feel you."

"Great," she says with an unconvincing smile. "Now, you've got about fifteen minutes to unpack before the campers arrive. There are three T-shirts under your pillow. You're expected to wear one whenever you're on duty. The towels are up at the bathroom, bug spray's on the windowsill. You'll figure out the rest as you go."

And just like that, J. Lo's evil twin disappears through the plastic curtain, and I'm left wondering how the hell I'm going to get myself out of here before she kills me.

Despite my fear of contracting a skin-eating disease, I plop down on the rickety cot and try to gather my thoughts. It's obvious that Dad isn't going to cave on this horrific wilderness experiment, but I'm practically an adult. Surely they can't keep me here against my will. I pop another peppermint into my mouth and chomp down on it. I need to talk to Katie. Her dad is a big-shot lawyer—if anyone will know how to get me out of here it's him.

I pull my phone from my bag, only to fall back into the pit of despair when I see there's absolutely no cell coverage. Freaking perfect.

Too pissed to cry, I start unloading my stuff before Fantine comes back and puts a cap in my ass. I'll figure out where AT&T lives later.

Using the strap of my bag to dust off the top shelf of the makeshift dresser, I lay my shorts, tanks, bras, and undies in neat piles on the wood, promising myself I'll burn them the second I get home. I swap my YSL tank for one of the standard-issue Hanes T-shirts, and finally trade out my flip-flops for the Asics trainers that have never set foot outside of a gym.

Looking like a walking yard sale, I return to the front entrance and find Fantine standing alongside Pete the doctor and Sam the gnome chef.

"All set?" Fantine asks. She's wearing a smile that I can't determine is of the sincere or I'm-going-to-kill-you-in-your-sleep variety.

"Yeah," I say cautiously. "Thanks."

I fall in line beside her and return a wave to Colin and Quinn, who are standing on the steps of the mess hall. Apparently my Quasimodo faux pas has been forgiven.

"Okay, gang." Rainbow approaches with a clipboard in hand and sunglasses stationed on her carrot-colored head. "The buses just radioed in. They're pulling off the highway and will be here in a couple of minutes."

"Finally," Fantine says. "I feel like we've been waiting forever."

"I know!" says Rainbow. She's so excited she's practically bouncing.

I'm just about to ask what the big deal is, when I notice Pete and Colin in an all-out hug, giggling like kids on Christmas morning. I'm beginning to wonder if I'm starring on a hidden camera reality show, because an eternity passes before two streaks of yellow finally appear through the thick of trees.

"Oh my God!" Fantine says while pressing her hands against her mouth. "They're here! They're here!"

"Don't you just love this?" Rainbow adds, squeezing her hand. "I cannot wait to see Meredith!"

Several minutes and a ridiculous amount of anticipation later, the buses roll to a stop in front of us. I squint behind my glasses, covering my nose and mouth from the dirt rising from the ground. Then the already too-familiar CAMP I CAN logo comes into view on the side of the bus.

A short bus.

I station myself at an equally safe distance from the squatty vehicles, watching as Rainbow waves wildly to the driver of the first bus, who responds with a heavy-handed honk. "I love it when he does that," she says. The engine goes silent and the dual glass doors at the front groan before squeaking open.

Fantine, Sam, and Pete have all wandered toward the other bus and are exchanging hellos with the driver, when a loud clanging noise draws my attention back to bus number one. A square door slowly opens from the side of the bus, creating an open-air lift. Seconds later a pigtailed redhead appears in the world's tiniest wheelchair.

"Hello, Raaaaaaainbow," the girl calls over in a voice that makes me think her tongue is too big for her mouth. "Did youuu miss meeee?"

"Did I miss you?" Rainbow bellows back. "Nah, never!"

The little girl answers with a laugh as strange as her voice, before her miniature body begins moving in ways that can't be good for you. Her hands are fisted, flailing in front of her face, while her neck contorts into an *Exorcist* move. I'm too freaked out to keep watching, so I turn my attention toward the other bus and find Fantine hugging a boy whose eyes are spaced entirely too far apart. His face is swollen, and I can't be sure, but it appears he's walking with a limp.

What the hell kind of freak show is this?

More yelping and laughter draws my awareness back to the first bus. The pigtailed, funny talker is now on the ground in her neon-yellow wheelchair (complete with an old-school Hannah Montana sticker plastered on its side). Then a dark-skinned boy with thick-lensed glasses sidesteps his way out of the bus, a pair of crutches in his hand.

And it dawns on me . . .

Oh. My. God. I'm spending my summer with a bunch of retards.

FOUR

"Cricket! Cricket, can you hear me?"

"Huh?" My eyes flutter open. Pete's freckled face is just inches from mine.

"Can you hear me?" he asks again, louder this time.

"Yes, Pete"—I wave him away with a swipe of my hand—"I can hear you. You don't need to yell in my face. What the hell happened?"

"You fainted, that's what happened. Can you try and sit up?"

"I think so."

Pete shimmies through the gravel and gently transitions me from lying flat on my back to propped up on my elbows.

"I feel a little . . ."

"Just take a few deep breaths and get your bearings. That was a pretty nasty fall."

I brace my elbows firmly into the dirt and hoist myself upright. The second I'm vertical, I drop my forehead against my knees. I haven't hurt like this since the morning after Tommy Kleeger's keg party.

"Any idea why you fainted?" I know he's just doing the whole bedside manner thing, but running his hand up and down my back isn't helping. "Are you dehydrated? When was the last time you ate?"

"It was probably the heat," I hear Fantine say. "She's probably only used to air-conditioning."

"I don't know what happened, just stop rubbing my back!" I say, wiggling away from Pete. "I've never been dehydrated before, so I don't know what that feels like, and it's not *that* hot. I have no idea why I fainted."

"Well, what's the last thing you remember?" Pete asks.

"I don't know. I . . . I guess I remember unpacking my stuff in the bunkhouse. . . ."

He nods. "That's good. What else?"

"Um . . . I remember waiting for the buses."

"Good, good. Keep going."

I'm just about to say, "I'm not a retard, Pete, you can shut up now," when a bright yellow object enters my peripheral vision, stealing my ability to speak. I glance over my shoulder and am immediately greeted with a picture of a prelesbian butch-cut Miley Cyrus and her enormous horse teeth.

"Are yooooou okay?"

I make a visor with my hand and squint up at the voice above me. The vision of two enormous pigtails sends my head into a tailspin as it all comes rushing back.

"Oh God," I mumble, burying my face in my knees.

"You remember now?" Pete asks.

"Oh yeah. I remember everything."

"Well, that's good to hear. What we need to do now is get you inside and out of the sun. Do you think you can stand up?"

"I can try."

"Okay, let's get you up on your feet. Quinn, can you take her on the left side please?"

"Yeah, sure."

Until this very moment I've only been aware that Pete, Fantine, and "Hannah Montana" are within range, but as I raise my head I see that a large crowd is circling, and yours truly is sitting center stage. There's a kid with an eye patch, another kid with drool trailing down his chin, and though I'm not sure who they belong to, a very BeDazzled pair of crutches sparkling in the sunlight. No wonder I fainted!

Before I can break into tears, Quinn approaches me. He looks as beautiful as I remembered, with the addition of a few worry lines etched in his forehead.

"You okay, Cricket?" he asks me quietly and kneels down. He drops his hand on my shoulder and our eyes meet. For an instant I forget I'm the lead float in the freak parade.

"I think so."

"Good. You had me worried for a minute." He flashes a quick smile that makes my insides somersault.

"All right, everybody," Rainbow says. Her distinct voice rips through my divine moment. "Dr. Pete is going to take good care of Cricket. You'll all have a chance to meet her after she rests up a bit. Now, everybody up to the mess hall!"

There's a brief round of cheers before the campers begin bumbling, rolling, and crutching their way up the hill toward the mess hall.

"You okay?" Fantine asks over her shoulder as she pushes Hannah Montana across the dirt. I nod, and she offers a smile that's a little easier to read this time. "Good," she says, honoring her word at giving me a second chance. "I'll check on you a little later. You guys take good care of her. She's not used to country life."

"We will. You ready over there, Quinn?" Pete asks as he wraps his arm around my shoulder and pulls me against him. I really don't think this level of assistance is necessary, but if it means Quinn will play human seat belt on the other side of me, I'm all for it.

"I'm ready." As hoped, Quinn repeats Pete's motion on my other side, securing his right hand around my waist. Under the circumstances, I know I shouldn't be enjoying this, but I just can't help myself.

"Well, a smile like that is a good sign. You must be feeling a little better," Pete says, as the three of us lumber up the hill toward the first-aid office.

"Yeah," I say. "Maybe a little."

✳ ✳ ✳

For the last half hour I've been laying on my aching, swollen ass with an ice pack on my head and a Lohan-size dose of Advil in my gut. My Hollywood heartthrob bailed about two seconds after we got here—thanks a lot, Quinn.

"Theriously, Pete," I say as he shoves the thermometer under my tongue again. "I don't have a feeva."

"Shhh," he says. "I'm still a med student. I haven't mastered thermometer-in-the-mouth language yet. It's a lot harder than it looks."

I'm too doped up on the graham crackers and warm apple juice Pete's been plying me with to give him a hard time. So instead I just flip him the bird.

"You're a spunky one, Cricket." His grin widens into a full smile as he pulls the thermometer from my mouth. "You were right. No feeva," he says, tossing the protective sleeve into the trash. "I think you're stable enough to return to work, so long as you promise you'll come back if your pain worsens or if you feel dizzy or light-headed, okay?"

I nod, though I have no intention of doing anything other than locating a cell signal. I slide my feet back into my tennies, make a quick adjustment to my ponytail, and fast-track to the door, when Pete offers up one last comment.

"It will change your life if you let it."

"Huh?"

"This camp," he clarifies. "I know it's a different summer job than lifeguarding or working at the Gap, but what we do here . . . well, it really means something. It's like we're part of something bigger than ourselves. If you allow yourself to enjoy it, and really experience what it's all about, I think you'll have one of the best summers of your life."

Oh please! The Gap?

"Look, Pete, if that's what works for you . . . great. But the only thing I'm looking to change this summer is my father's mind about leaving me here. Otherwise, I intend to remain exactly the same person I've always been. Thanks for the ice."

"No problem," he says easily enough. "Just remember you promised to come back if you need to."

"Right," I call over my shoulder before pulling the thin wooden door shut behind me.

I slide my sunglasses back into place and quickly survey my surroundings. Hallelujah! Not a crippled soul in sight. Without hesitation, I haul ass back to the bunk house, grab my phone, and take off down a broken path that leads away from camp. I know my cellular liberation is out there—I just need to find it!

It's embarrassing how quickly I run out of breath. Within minutes, I'm hunched over, shuffling along the path while my phone searches for service.

"Come on, come on"—I tap my finger impatiently against the screen—"just give me a bar. Please, just one freaking ba—"

The distinct sound of leaves being crunched silences me. With very slow movements, I raise my head and look in the direction I think the noise came from. It's only now that I realize things don't look the same as they did when I started this little quest. I'm no longer in a maintained campground area peppered with outbuildings and designated paths. Instead I'm surrounded by boulders and scraggly brush. And it's sort of dark. Why is it dark in the middle of the day? I brave a look upward; my pulse quickening. Besides the few beams of dusty sunlight creeping in through the thick trees, I might as well be in a tomb. Or a bad horror movie.

A thorny bush just a few yards from me begins to shake, its tiny leaves crackling like dry wood on a campfire from whatever is leaning into it. I swallow back the knot of fear that's suddenly wedged itself in my throat.

"Shhh. You'll scare it away."

I jump. The sound of another voice more than startles me, and I stumble backward while tripping over a rock in the process.

"Oh, geez! Cricket, are you okay?"

Heart still pounding out of control with pain radiating up my legs, I whip my head over my shoulder. It takes me a moment to recognize that it's Quinn running toward me and not a serial killer.

"I'm so sorry," he says, already at my side and surveying my injury. "I didn't mean to scare you. I just didn't want you to miss seeing her."

"Her?" I stare up at him, confusion already overriding my sense of fear.

"Yeah," he says. "Look."

I follow the point of his finger over my shoulder and catch the tail end of a deer leaping through the bushes.

"Oh my God!" I'm not sure if I should laugh or cry. "It was a freaking deer!"

He laughs. "Yeah, pretty cool, right?"

"Totally cool," I say, trying my best not to sound awkward.

"Again, I really am sorry. Are you sure you're okay?"

"Yeah, I think so." Quinn stands up first and offers me his hand for assistance, which I waste no time accepting.

"You're not off to such a great start here," he says, motioning to my legs. I look down to see streams of blood trailing down both shins. "Are you notoriously accident-prone or is this just a particularly bad day?"

"I don't know." I feel my cheeks redden. "A little bit of both, I guess. I gave myself a black eye with the refrigerator door once; it's why I don't snack in the middle of the night anymore. And last year I tripped over our dog and broke three toes on my right foot. But, otherwise, I think I'm pretty stable."

The corner of his mouth begins to twitch. "What kind of dog was it?"

"A beagle. His name is Mr. Katz."

"Mr. Katz," he says, sounding amused. He relaxes his stance

against a tree. "That's a cool name. What happened to poor Mr. Katz?"

"He died."

"Oh man, I'm sorry. . . ."

"I'm just kidding," I say, easing my weight against a neighboring rock as I start to feel more relaxed. "You could drive a truck over that dog and he wouldn't die. He's got some weird doggy superpower or something. Anyway," I change gears before I start rambling again. "Why are you out here?"

"I saw you leave Pete's cabin and wanted to make sure you were feeling all right. When I didn't see you at the girls' dorm, I figured you were out exploring."

Exploring. Right.

"So, is it safe to assume that was your first encounter with a deer?"

I nod. "I thought for sure it was an escaped serial killer."

"You did?"

"Yeah. Until you showed up and scared the crap out of me. Then I thought you were the killer."

He laughs, and I notice that his bottom teeth aren't perfectly straight—a quality I usually frown upon, but on him it's surprisingly cute. "Well, I really am sorry," he says. "Believe it or not, I try not to make a habit out of scaring people. At least not on their first day." Now it's my turn to laugh. Conversations with boys are never this easy. "So what were you really doing out here? Looking for an escape route?"

And so much for easy conversation.

"What do you mean?" I say.

He points to my phone.

"Oh yeah. I was just . . . going to see if we get any coverage. My dad will be wondering if I got here okay, and my best friend Katie . . . well, she can't go more than an hour without talking to me."

"Uh-huh," he says, fighting another grin. "And you're sure it doesn't have anything to do with Fantine?"

My head tilts to one side as I consider a question I wasn't prepared for. He thinks I want to escape because of Fantine?

"Look, I don't pretend to understand why girls do the things they do, but for the most part she's a pretty cool chick. She's been saddled with the new counselors the last couple of years and they seem to be getting worse and worse, although I'm sure you'll buck the trend. If she throws attitude at you, don't take it personally."

Note to self: now is definitely not the time to tell Quinn that wheelchairs far outrank Fantine on my Things That Scare Cricket list.

"I think she's going to kill me in my sleep."

His grin stretches into a full smile. Apparently I'm amusing.

"Well, if she does make an attempt on your life, scream really loud. Our cabin's not that far from yours. Although I sleep like the dead, so the odds of me hearing you aren't in your favor." I can't help but smile. A sleeping Quinn is a nice visual. "In the meantime, there's a phone in the mess hall that you're allowed to use. Just dial nine to get an outside line. But as far as the cell goes, if you climb up by that water tower over there"—he pushes away from the tree and leans in close to me, pointing to a hill a few hundred yards away—"you should be able to get service."

I catch the faint scent of cinnamon on his breath and have to swallow hard before I can respond. "Thanks. I'll keep that in mind."

Neither of us move for a moment, and though we're not looking at each other, I can't help but wonder if he's feeling the same thing I am. That there's a connection between us that feels . . . electric.

"It looks like you need to make a trip back to Pete's office," he says suddenly, stepping away from me to survey my knee again. "It probably just needs some Neosporin and a couple of Band-Aids, but you really should let him check you out."

So much for electricity.

"Yeah, you're probably right."

"Come on." He motions toward camp. "I'll make sure Pete fixes you up, and then we'll head down to the lower field to meet everybody."

Crap. Ten minutes with Zac Efron's doppelgänger and I almost forgot where I was.

"Right. Meet everybody. . . ."

"Don't worry," he says coolly. "Everybody will love you."

Though it's not *everybody* I'm hoping for. . . .

✳ ✳ ✳

"See, that wasn't so bad," Pete says.

I look down at my knees to find two gigantic yellow Band-Aids covered with face shots of Edward Cullen and the rest of his immortal family. "You can't be serious. I can't walk around with these on my legs."

"Why not? I heard they were really good books."

"Oh my God. Can you help me out here?" I look beyond Pete's full-blown grin to the other side of the room where Quinn is perched on an empty milk crate. His arms are crossed over his chest, and there's not a hint of emotion on his face.

"I don't know what to tell you, Cricket," he says with a shrug. "According to every magazine at the grocery store, that guy is the hottest guy on the planet. I'd think you'd enjoy having his mug plastered across your body."

I want to laugh, but there's no way I'm giving either of them the satisfaction. "You two are real a-holes, you know that?"

"Well, I can see if I have a *High School Musical* one down in the depths of the drawer here, but it'll be old and probably won't stick very well." Pete spins around on his doctor stool, and now I can't help but laugh. Quinn has suddenly ditched his cool act, and is halfway out the door.

"Come on, Cricket," he calls back to me. "Time for us to go. See ya later, Pete."

"Ah, come on dude." Pete is now laughing harder than me. "You've gotta learn to embrace your inner Efron."

"Yeah, Quinn, embrace your inner Efron!" I say, surprising myself by joining in on the banter.

Quinn flips Pete and me a tanned middle finger, while I hop off the table and stumble toward the door laughing. If only camp consisted of hanging out with these two all day.

"Thanks, Pete," I say. "I'm sure I'll be back in a couple of hours with a new injury. Maybe you can hook me up with a Troy Band-Aid next time."

"I'm pretty sure Troy Band-Aids are extinct, but I do have a few fancy Biebers to choose from. Or a Littlest Pet Shop if that's more your style."

"Pet shop," I say. A girl's gotta have standards.

I follow Quinn out the door, and feel my amusement fading when I realize that we're alone again.

"You don't really mind the comparison to Efron, do you?"

"I don't know," he says a little sheepishly. "It's not so bad now that he's older and people take him more seriously, but I was only in eighth grade when *High School Musical* came out. Do you know how crazy middle school girls can be?" I have to laugh. I was in sixth grade when that movie came out—I know damn well how crazy middle school girls can be. "They were stopping me for pictures, asking me for autographs—"

"Do they still ask you for autographs?"

"Sometimes."

"And do you actually sign his name?"

"Nah. I just sign my own name really sloppy. I figure they won't know the difference."

"That's pretty awesome." As I say this, I see his sapphire gaze travel to my hands. Somehow they've gone and wrapped themselves around his arm.

"Hey, you two!"

Oh, for the love of God. I pry my eyes—and hands—from Quinn the moment Rainbow comes into range. She's just feet from us with two mesh bags of sporting equipment thrown over each shoulder. "Are you feeling any better, Cricket?"

I want to say, "I was until you showed up," but all I come up with is a nod.

"Glad to hear it. Would you guys mind taking these bags down to the lower field while I get Sam started on dinner? Colin says they're eager to start playing and they just cannot *wait* to meet you, Cricket!"

Oh boy.

"Sure thing," Quinn answers easily. He must be immune to the grating quality of her voice after all these years. "We definitely don't want to mess with dinner."

I take the smaller of the two bags and heave it over my

shoulder with a grunt. Unlike me, Quinn doesn't seem at all irritated with the idea of doing manual labor.

"I hope I didn't offend you back there," he says, once Rainbow's out of earshot and we're alone again.

"What are you talking about?"

"When I was saying how crazy middle school girls can be. For all I know *you* asked me for my autograph."

I laugh. "Not likely. Troy was cute, but Captain Jack was the only man in my life in middle school."

"Johnny Depp?" He reels his head back. "No way."

"Yeah way. He's hot."

"Johnny Depp?" he asks again, still sounding shocked.

"Yes. Johnny Depp."

"But he's so . . . old," he says. "And short."

"Dude, I'm not recruiting him to play basketball. I just liked him as that character. He was unique and quirky and mysterious all at once. Plus he rocked the black eye liner. Most guys can't pull that off."

He considers this for what seems like a while, before slowly shaking his head. "I will never understand girls."

The smile that stretches across my face is as genuine as any I've ever felt, and takes me by surprise. Four hours ago I never would have imagined I'd be enjoying myself. But I am. For this moment, anyway.

FIVE

"Cricket's here! Cricket's here!"

Before I can even ditch my load of playground balls, I'm attacked by a blonde girl whose smashed-in face strongly resembles a Pekingese.

"What are you doing!" I say, dropping the bag and raising my arms like she's carrying a rare infectious disease.

"Cricket, this is Claire," Fantine says, coming to my rescue by gently easing the human leech from my body. "Claire is going to be in your group this summer."

She can't be serious. I turn to Quinn, hoping for some sort of salvation, but he's looking just as stoked over this meet 'n greet as Fantine and Claire. "Um . . . hello, Claire," I say, determining this is not the time to tell her she looks like a dog. "It's . . . nice to meet you. I'm Cricket."

"Duh! We know who you are. You fainted."

Either my fainting spell was funnier than I remember, or Claire is the resident comedienne. Every wonky-eyed freak in sight is laughing like it's the funniest thing they've ever heard.

Recognizing my obvious unease, Quinn strides over with an

easy look on his face. He squats down beside me.

"You're right, Claire, she fainted, but she's fine now. Dr. Pete took good care of her. You see, he even gave her these supercool Band-Aids."

"Oh! I love vampires." Before I can retreat, she drops to her dimpled knees for a better look. "I love Edward," she explains while I shoot eye daggers at Quinn. "His skin is cold all the time, but his orange eyes are so pretty! Do you love his eyes, Cricket?"

"Uh . . . yeah, I guess."

"Bella loves Edward's eyes, too. And his lips—she's *always* kissing him."

I'm about to ask for an intervention on the *Twilight* love fest going on at my feet, when Claire leans forward and plants a kiss squarely on Edward Cullen's scowling face. "There you go. Your knee is all better now."

Oh. My. God. Which way to the acid bath?

"I see you've met Claire." Rainbow appears, wearing her same jolly expression. "Let's introduce you to the rest of the crew, and then we'll play a game of kickball before dinner. Does that sound good?"

Through the eruption of cheers, animalistic yelps, and a very unexpected, "Piss! Piss, cockin' balls!" by a kid who looks like a *Big Bang Theory* extra, I begin to rethink my original opinion of this place. Circus sideshow? Hell yeah. A cult? No way. Even the most jacked-up religions have criteria for membership.

"Whatever," I say.

Wearing a huge, stupid grin, Rainbow introduces me to the remaining campers: Six boys and four more girls ranging from thirteen to fifteen years old. At least I think that's what they said. It's tough to be sure since each of them speaks with a slur, stutter, or some other speech defect. I feign interest as best I can without gagging, but it isn't until Rainbow announces that *I'm* going to be in charge of the end-of-summer battle of the bands that I actually start to pay attention.

"I'm supposed to do *what?*"

"You're going to be in charge of the show," she says in a tone that's almost as exhausted as the expression on her face. "Your father didn't explain this to you before you got here?"

"Sorry to disappoint you, but my dad explained absolutely nothing about this place. And I mean *nothing.*"

She studies my face, the creases next to her eyes deepening with every passing second. "Come with me," she says.

I deliver a hearty eye-roll in Quinn's direction before catching up with her under a cluster of pine trees.

"Look, Cricket," she says. "I was under the impression that you knew this was a camp for special needs kids. I'm sorry you didn't, but now that you do, I really need you to step up to the plate and pull your weight. Besides being the lead counselor for Claire and Meredith, you're going to be coordinating the battle of the bands. It's not *American Idol* or anything—each counselor puts together a routine with their campers and then there's one big group number that you'll be in charge of—but it's a big deal to the kids and their parents."

Besides the fact that I don't plan to be here longer than twenty-four hours, I don't know the first thing about coordinating a live show. I was a cheerleader, not a drama dork.

"How the hell could I possibly make a show out of . . . that?" I motion toward the campers.

I see her jaw bone clinch beneath her gummy complexion. "You're a smart girl," she says after sucking in a deep breath. "You'll figure out what to do. I think once you settle in and get to know everybody, you'll find it's a lot of fun."

"Are you kidding me? How is spending two weeks with a bunch of handicapped kids fun? I can't even understand what they're saying! This isn't fun, this is . . . it's a short bus nightmare!"

"That's enough!" she says. By the expression on her face you'd think I just popped her in the gut. "From the moment you stepped out of that car you've acted like an insolent, spoiled brat and I won't have you behaving that way around these kids. You need to get your act together or I'm going to have to call your father, and he won't be happy to hear how you've been behaving."

It takes every ounce of self-control in my body not to laugh in her face. Why does every adult think that threatening kids with a bad report card is going to scare us into changing?

"You don't have a clue what you're talking about," I say. I

manage to ward off the laughter, but there's no way I can stop my eyes from rolling. "My dad may have been pissed enough to send me here—but trust me, he still thinks the world revolves around me."

"Is that so?"

Her insinuation ignites an unfamiliar response in me: the need to defend my relationship with my dad. Current nightmare aside, we get along just fine. We may not get all Dr. Phil with deep conversations, but it's always worked for us.

"Yeah," I say. "It is. He may have sent me here to learn some kind of lesson, but he knew exactly how I'd react when I got here. And because he knows me so well, he'd also know that I have no intention of sitting back while my summer is ruined."

This forces her to take a step back. "So what are you saying? You're thinking of leaving?"

"Obviously."

"Oh . . . oh dear." The anger quickly dissolves from her face and she's looking at me all hollow-cheeked and saggy, like a balloon with a slow leak. "Well, I guess you have a choice to make then. Do you want to stay or go?"

I glance over my shoulder, ignoring Quinn's quizzical stare, and take in the eleven *special* kids I'm expected to transform into Simon Cowell's next boner.

"Decision made. I'm outta here."

SIX

I run for what feels like hours while tears stream down my face. I fly past the bunkhouse and bathroom, hardly breaking stride when I weave my way through the narrow pathway where I met the deer. I have no concern for the thorny bushes attacking my legs, the rock in my shoe, or serial killers hiding in the shadows.

I manage to reach the bottom of the hill Quinn told me about and yank my phone from my back pocket. The display still says NO NETWORK. I grunt out an exhausted breath, blowing wisps of sweaty hair from my face, and look up at the steep path that winds to the top of the hill. Under normal circumstances I wouldn't even consider climbing something this high. Hell, I couldn't even make it to the top of the cheer-pyramid sophomore year. But this isn't a normal circumstance—this is about cellular salvation!

An eternity passes before I finally make it to the top. I'm too amped at the three bars showing on the display to care that I'm covered in dirt and sweating like a pig, or that there's fresh blood dripping down my right leg.

I punch number one on the speed dial before collapsing against the hard-packed earth. The faint sound of the phone ringing is so sweet I almost start crying again.

"Oh my God!" Katie answers. "I've been trying to call you, but it keeps dumping me into voice mail. Where are you?"

"I'm in hell!" I shriek, wiping back a tear. "Handicapped hell!"

"You're where? Wait . . . what?"

"I'm at a camp for handicapped kids in Michigan! I had to climb a freaking mountain just to call you!"

"Oh my God! You've *got* to be kidding me."

"I swear to God," I say, rolling onto my back.

"Oh, this is epic, Crick. Seriously. You're hanging out with a bunch of 'tards instead of hitting the beach—are you like totally ready to hang yourself?"

"Obviously!" Growing frustrated with this pointless back and forth, I cut to the chase. "We have to figure out how to get me out of here, Katie."

". . . Okay."

"Well?"

"Well what? What do you expect me to do? I'm leaving for Maui in the morning, in case you forgot. I haven't packed a thing."

"How could I forget? I was supposed to go with you!"

"Oh my God, I almost forgot. Remember that suede Burberry bag, the yellow sling back with the metallic studs? My mom got it for me for the trip—"

"Are you kidding me right now? I don't give a shit about metallic studs, Katie. I need to get out of here!"

"Okay, okay. God, chill. What do you want me to do?"

"Talk to your dad. They have to be breaking some laws by holding me here against my will. I'm practically a hostage. Maybe he can call the director and scare her with some of his legal talk."

"Dude, your dad did this. It's not like we can file an Amber Alert when your own parent is the one who ditched you." I have to grind my teeth to keep from screaming. Of all the times for my best friend to go traitor on me. "*Your* dad is your ticket out of there, Crick. Not mine."

I heave a deep breath.

"I know," I say reluctantly. "But I don't see how I'm going to convince him."

"He'll cave."

"I'm not so sure. I've never seen him like that before, Katie. He was just so . . ."

"Pissed? So what. Parents are always pissed at their kids."

Actually, I was going to say disappointed.

"Cricket, this is your dad we're talking about. The same guy who bought you a brand-new car a week after you totaled the first one. The same man who grounded you for a month only to renege on it two days later because you started to cry. Do you honestly think he's going to leave you to rot in the woods for two whole weeks?"

"I don't know . . ."

"He's not going to. As soon as he gets back from his trip, he'll come and get you. He's just trying to make a point."

I'm not fully convinced, but I agree anyway.

"When does he get home?"

I do a quick mental count of Dad's travel schedule. "Oh my God . . . that's eight days! There's no way I can do eight days of this."

"Oh please," she says, doing little to hide the are-you-done-yet in her voice. "Are you telling me there's absolutely nothing there that can occupy your time for a week?"

I'm just about to respond, "Have you even been listening to me?" when out of nowhere, a familiar silhouette approaches me through the setting sun. His stride is so easy and confident I can't help but smile.

"Now that you mention it, there is something here that could be a good distraction."

"Ooh, I know that voice. How hot is he?"

"*Very*," I say cautiously, as Quinn is now a few feet away from me. I shield my eyes with my hand to look up at him, nearly melting at the grin he fires back. "Call me when you get to Maui. Hopefully I'll have some news to report." I power down before Katie can dive into one of her diatribes about the importance of dating a guy who is good-looking but not better-looking than you (she reads a lot of *Cosmo*) and stare up at my visitor.

"I thought I might find you up here. Can I sit?"

"Sure."

He sets a paper sack down on the ground before settling in

beside me. At least a foot separates us, but I can still feel the warmth from his body.

"Not bad, huh?"

By the motion of his head I know he's referring to the view of the darkening valley below us, but I can't take my eyes off him. "Not bad at all," I say.

"So it sounds like you were able to find some coverage. Is your friend surviving without you?"

"Oh yeah. It turns out a trip to Maui is all she needs to get over me being gone. I was supposed to go with her, you know."

"Really? I've never been. Is it as nice as they say?"

"I guess it depends on who *they* are. My dad thinks it's over-rated—he prefers more exotic locations, but I love it. White sands, warm water . . . it's like taking a bath all day."

"Sounds like paradise."

"Yeah."

"Definitely not like western Michigan."

"Exactly. Oh no, I didn't mean . . ."

"I'm just kidding," he says with a laugh, leaning into my arm. "I'd rather be in Hawaii than here, too. Well, not *here* per se, but anyway . . . Rainbow said you were thinking about leaving?"

"No!" My immediate answer surprises us both. "I mean, I don't think I could even if I wanted to." Not for the next eight days, anyway. "My dad's out of the country and he's the only person that could do anything about it. I think I'm just going to have to suck it up for a while."

"Suck it up, huh? So you really were looking for a way to escape earlier."

"Uh . . ."

"Relax, I'm not judging. This isn't the kind of place most people can just drop right into and feel at home. This is my fourth summer here, and I still have my moments where I feel a little out of place."

"Seriously?"

"Seriously," he says. "We all do. You'll have to ask Colin about Scotty Marshall sometime. That is a perfect example of how crazy things can be around here. I swear that was one of the funniest things I've ever seen."

"Well?"

"Nah"—he shakes his head—"I can't. Colin has earned the right to tell that story. Just make sure you ask him."

I have no idea what he's talking about, but a sudden image of Colin and his huge smile drifts through my mind. "Okay," I say. "I'll ask him."

Our conversation about Colin dies out like a forgotten camp-fire, and before long, we find ourselves in a moment of silence. Considering we've only known each other a few hours, this should probably feel awkward, but it doesn't. It's strangely comfortable.

"What's in the bag?" I ask, peeking over him.

"Oh, I almost forgot. I brought you dinner." He reaches into the brown sack, producing a triangular shaped piece of tinfoil. He carefully unfolds the wrapping and presents two slices of pizza. "Friday nights are all about pizza and movies."

I don't typically eat in front of guys I'm hoping to kiss (another of Katie's *Cosmo* rules), but considering the only thing I've eaten all day were Pete's soggy graham crackers and some peppermints, I don't hesitate to dive in.

"Wow," I say, pausing only long enough to breathe. "This is so good. Where'd you get it?"

"Sam made it. He cooks all the food here."

I nearly choke. "Seriously? Sam made this? Sam who doesn't speak in complete sentences?"

"Yep"—he nods, trying not to laugh as I manhandle my dinner—"he's an incredible chef. He studied at a culinary institute in New York."

"*Sam?*"

"Yes, Sam. Hard to believe?"

"Well, yeah actually. It is. Isn't there something, I mean, obviously there's something different. . . ."

"Sam's autistic," he says, the word rolling off his tongue like he says it every day. "He's sort of like Rain Man. He's got an exceptional memory, but not for everything. Well, not for most things, really. When it comes to cooking or anything to do with Madonna, the guy's like an encyclopedia. But everything else goes in one ear and out the other."

"That sucks."

"Eh, I don't know. I think it's a lot like Maui. It depends on who you ask."

"Huh?" I grunt, popping the last of the pizza into my mouth. "How do you figure?"

"He doesn't know any different. It would suck for us because we know what a normal life is like, but he doesn't. It's just how he's always been. I think it's the same thing with the campers. Other than Aidan, they've always been the way they are."

"Are they all um . . . what did you call it?"

"Autistic? No. None of them are, actually. The kids here either have a Down's syndrome or cerebral palsy diagnosis—and they're all high-functioning at that. There are special camps specifically for kids with autism since their needs are very different. They need lots of structure and really specific routines. We're too laid-back for them."

"Laid-back. Right," I mumble, though not as quietly as planned, because he laughs at me. "What?" I say.

"Nothing. We better get going if we want to make it down the hill with some light. The movie starts at eight sharp, and I'm guessing you might want to clean up first."

I glace at my arms and legs, then immediately cover my face with equally dirty hands. All this time I've been sitting here looking like one of Brad and Angelina's rescue projects.

"Don't worry, you're allowed to get messy at camp. Nobody

will think you're any less beautiful."

I fight back a nervous giggle as his compliment ricochets through my brain. Maybe eight days in hell won't be as bad as I thought.

Quinn offers his hand to help me up. I'm not surprised to find that it's warm and carries that same electric current I felt earlier. I take a breath as he pulls me to my feet, and then I realize that this is the perfect moment. The sun is dropping in the distance, the trees are casting long shadows across the ground, and the warm summer breeze is blowing my hair. Now he just needs to kiss me.

My heart begins to race as he squeezes my hand before narrowing his gaze on my mouth. *Cosmo* would say we're moving too fast, but I don't give a crap about big sister advice. I allow my eyes to drift shut, prepping myself for what is bound to be the best first kiss ever, when he says, "You've got a little pizza sauce right here."

My eyes flutter open. "What?"

"Right here." He dabs at my cheek with the same hand I had been holding seconds before. "It was so good you were saving some for later?"

I feel my cheeks warm with embarrassment as I scrub at the leftover sauce. "Thanks," I say with false amusement. "I guess I'm a bigger mess than I realized."

"Yeah, maybe you are," he says, leaning close enough so I can see my reflection in his eyes. "But that's when life starts getting good, right? When it's messy."

SEVEN

"There's no way I can do this," I whisper to Fantine the next morning. "I'm supposed to be their counselor and I don't have a clue how to communicate with them. They all sound like they've swallowed their tongues. And what's with that kid, Trevor? His left eye points in a completely different direction than the right one. It's creepy!"

She rolls her eyes while shimmying her long toned legs into a pair of cutoffs. "Take a breath already. You heard what Rainbow said last night. Since battle of the bands isn't until the last night of camp, you don't have to start rehearsals right away. You'll tag along with me for a few days, get to know everybody, and then we'll incorporate the show into their schedules. You'll have tons of time to get it all worked out—it's no big deal. Besides, I think you did pretty good last night."

I think back momentarily to the chaos that was the night before. After Quinn returned me to my bunk, I took a quick shower, changed clothes, swiped my lashes for good measure, and joined everyone at the mess hall for movie night.

Rainbow cornered me the second I stepped foot on the cracked linoleum floor.

"I wasn't able to reach your father," she said in a quiet, yet firm voice. "According to your housekeeper, he's out of the country until a week from tomorrow. Since you don't have another legal guardian who can give me permission to let you leave, you'll have to stay."

Well, there's a news flash, Anderson Cooper.

The campers may have been too preoccupied with their microwave popcorn to notice our conversation, but it definitely didn't get past my fellow counselors. I turned my back to them for more privacy. "I guess I don't have a choice then, do I?"

"Does this mean you'll give it a shot?"

I looked sadly at my flip-flopped feet. My once-beautiful toes looked like I'd taken a jackhammer to them. And thanks to some blisters from my seldom worn Asics, each pinkie toe was sporting a shimmery red Bieber Band-Aid. It was all so sad. And yet, there I was, actually agreeing to do it.

"I guess," I finally said. "But I'm still planning to call my dad the second he's back in town."

A smile spread across her speckled face, and for a moment I thought she might cry. "I'll let the rest of the team know what you've decided. I have a good hunch you'll want to stay."

"Don't hold your breath."

Rainbow disappeared into the kitchen with an unsettling spring in her step, while I stood completely dumbfounded, wondering what the hell I'd just done. Colin finally broke me from my fog when he stood in front of the group and announced that the movie of our night was the original *Karate Kid*. (There was an original?) I selected a spot on a fuzzy green pillow next to Fantine's blue one, praying that Quinn would occupy the other side and the campers would stay at least five arms' lengths away.

That lasted for all of four seconds. . . .

"Chirp, chirp! Where is Cricket? Chirp, chirp!" Claire suddenly appeared by my side, crouching in a position I wasn't certain she'd ever get out of. "Quinn said you will sit with me."

"What?"

She leaned forward and whispered right against my ear. "Quinn said you will sit with me."

I jerked back. "No, um, you must have misunderstood—" Before I could assure her that sitting anywhere near me was not an option, she plopped her enormous, disproportionate body onto the other half of my pillow. She proceeded to tell me, *again*, how much she loved Robert Pattinson, and that even though her parents assured her otherwise, she was pretty sure vampires actually did exist.

Trying to ignore her, I searched the room for Quinn. I found him sitting on a metal folding chair with his feet crossed at his ankles and a devious smile resting on his otherwise perfect face.

"What the hell?" I mouthed, raising my hands.

His only response was an exaggerated shrug.

I was about to return the middle finger salute he gave me

earlier in the day, when a heavy poke on my shoulder forced me to turn back to Claire.

"What now?" I said.

"Meredith doesn't like Edward."

"Meredith? Who the hell is Meredith?"

"Her," Claire says, motioning behind me.

I craned my neck over my right shoulder and nearly shrieked when I found the wheel-chaired, Hannah Montana stalker just inches from my face.

"Mom saaaaaays vampires aren't reeeeal," Meredith sputtered. "Are they reeeeal, Cricket?"

"Chirp! Chirp!" Claire added. "Are they, Cricket?"

Both girls broke into a fit of laughter, while I turned to Fantine, hoping she would offer me some sort of salvation. Like maybe a rock to the head.

"Looks like you've got some new friends," she said, making no attempt to hide her amusement.

"Can't you move them? Or roll them somewhere? This is a huge room, is there nowhere else they can sit?"

Fantine motioned her head back toward the pair who were getting even more comfortable in their respective seats. *My* seat. "I think they're pretty happy where they are. Besides, they're both in love with Zac Efron over there. He tells them to sit with you, they're gonna do it."

I looked beyond her and found that Quinn had moved from

the folding chair to a black beanbag just a few feet away. Sitting Indian style on his right side was the black kid with superthick glasses I saw climbing off the bus, his crutches a few feet away on the floor. On his left, squatting like he was hoping to lay an egg, was the kid I only remembered as the Drooler.

The Drooler got to sit beside Quinn, and I was stuck with my new BFFs. WTF?

I edged to the corner of my cushion with my eyes fixed on the screen, and silently prayed for the gates of hell to open up and take me already.

Just as Quinn said, the movie started rolling at eight on the dot, but it took at least fifteen minutes before the Wonder Twins beside me finally shut up and stopped laughing. Other than random outbursts of "balls," "cock," or "piss" by a red-haired boy named Chase, the room was virtually silent. It wasn't until the final scene, when Daniel-san did his famous crane kick to defeat the sexy Cobra Kai bully, when the gates of hell actually did come flying open.

Claire saw me sucking back tears, a reaction I'm sure everyone has the first time they see that movie, and felt the need to share my sentiments with the entire room.

"Cricket loves Daniel-san, Cricket loves Daniel-san!" She was singing at the top of her lungs, hopping around like a frog with broken legs. I was half a breath away from telling her to shut her crazy pie-hole, when Meredith and her ten-thousand-pound wheelchair rolled over my hand.

"Son of a bitch!" I shook my hand, hoping to regain feeling. But my need for medical attention was quickly dismissed in the midst of the chaos going on around me.

"Waaaaax on, Cricket! Waaaaax off, Cricket!" Meredith yelled from her wheelchair, while Trevor with the freaky eyes added, "Don't forget to breathe!" Within a minute every window-licker within a thousand feet was jumping, hobbling, rolling, or bouncing through the room shrieking about my love for the Karate Kid.

High-functioning my ass—those kids were freakin' nuts!

"Damn, that was funny," Fantine says, bringing me back to the present with a hearty laugh.

"I'm still not sure how I got out of there without a tranquilizer gun," I say, and find I'm actually laughing with her. "You guys didn't help any, either. Pete said he almost wet his pants."

"I'm pretty sure he did. He took off and didn't tell anybody where he went—probably had to change into some clean boxers."

I blow out a heavy sigh as the memory of the night before slowly disappears and the reality of my day comes back into light. "I'm thrilled to have been part of your entertainment for the evening, but I still don't think I can do this. It's no big deal when you guys are around, but I'm going to have to be alone with them at some point. I just don't think I can pull it off."

"They're just kids, Cricket. They don't bite. At least not most of them," she says, dropping her head between her knees as she pulls her penny-colored curls into a ponytail. "Are they different?

Yes. Will there be times when you think you're going crazy? *Hell* yes. But once you get over that stuff, you'll actually have a good time. Besides"—she flips back up with a crude smile on her face—"I saw you eyeing Quinn more than a couple times last night. If you leave early, you won't be getting any action."

"Ugh, whatever."

"Oh, I'm sorry," she says dramatically. "It must be the other Barbie twin whose eyes glaze over the minute he walks into the room."

"They do not!" I say, a little too emphatically to believe. "I just think he's cute. That's all. I mean, he looks like a celebrity!"

She crosses her muscular arms over her chest and glares at me. "So the fact that he's sweet as pie, earned a scholarship, *and* bends it like Beckham doesn't factor into your opinion of him whatsoever? Not one little bit?"

I chew on my lip, fearing that if I try to speak I'll burst into hysterics.

"Mmm-hmm, that's what I thought," she says. "Come on, Mrs. Efron, let's get these girls ready for breakfast."

* * *

Never in my life did I think teenage girls could spend an entire Saturday without a trip to Barney's, marathon texting, or a Liam Hemsworth movie, but that's exactly what happened today. And I hated every minute of it.

From the very awkward breakfast where I was wedged between my two self-proclaimed BFFs, Claire and Meredith, to diving for cover when wonky-eyed Trevor misjudged his archery target by about nine thousand feet, I hadn't had a moment's peace all day. (FYI: Archery lessons have been cancelled for the rest of the summer. Ya think!) Even tonight's amazing shrimp scampi was ruined when Robyn, one of Fantine's bobble-headed campers, threw up all over my new Kors denim shorts. Not even a full Quinn grin could make a food allergy puke fest less revolting. As far as I was concerned, my dad's return to the States couldn't come soon enough.

It wasn't until we'd finished dinner and I bagged my new shorts in a Hefty that things started looking up.

"Did anybody tell you what we do on Saturday nights?"

I can't help but roll my eyes at Fantine's question. Had she completely forgotten that besides her, my interactions with anyone with half an IQ point was virtually nonexistent?

"No," I say. "Somehow I missed the news flash about the wild and crazy Saturday nights at Camp Kill Me Now."

"Stop being so freaking dramatic," she says. "Saturday nights we sing songs, roast s'mores, tell ghost stories around the campfire—"

"Sounds riveting."

"My God, you're annoying sometimes," she continues, proving my death glare has nothing on hers. "As I was saying, after we do all that and get the kids settled for the night, the four of us get to go out."

"What!" I scramble off the bed. "Did you say we get to go out? Like, away from here?"

"I thought that would get your attention."

She drops down beside me so we're both sitting on the edge of my bed. In a quiet voice she says, "As long as there isn't anything serious going on here, Rainbow will cover things at our cabin and Pete will cover things at the boys'. She doesn't care when we get back, as long as we're up and ready in time for breakfast."

"Where will we go? What will we do?"

"There's a little town called Freeport about twenty minutes north of here," she says. I scootch closer, hanging on every word like she's Jesus delivering the Sunday sermon. "There's not a whole lot to do, but there's a bowling alley and a Denny's. It's better than nothing."

I have no idea what this Denny's is, but I already know it's going to be perfect.

"Colin's also twenty-one now," she adds. "So I'm sure he'll hook us up with some beer. Do you drink?"

"Sometimes. At parties or whatever. Do you?"

"Same, but we can't drink much. If Rainbow suspects we've been drinking, we'll be fired on the spot. No exceptions."

Fired on the spot, eh? The proverbial light bulb in my brain flickers on.

Hello, escape route.

EIGHT

or the record, a Saturday night should never involve burned s'mores, Scooby-Doo-inspired ghost stories, or off-key renditions of the same Taylor Swift song sung so many times one considers ripping off their own ears with a pair of pliers. If not for the drunken liberation awaiting me, suicide would sound like a pretty legit course of action right now.

At ten o'clock, we start herding the campers to bed.

"Just a few more minutes," Fantine says under her breath, while subtly tapping the face of her watch.

"Believe me, I know." Despite our differing motivations, it's nice to know I'm not the only one eager to get the hell out of here.

"Cricket?" A hearty tug on my arm forces my attention away from Fantine to my right side. Oh goody, it's Claire. "You're tucking us in, right?"

"*What?*"

Per usual, Claire thinks I didn't hear her question, when in reality I'm too disgusted by it to answer. "You're tucking us in, right?" she says again, motioning to herself and Meredith, who has just wheeled up beside her.

"You're kidding, right?"

They shake their heads.

"Aren't you guys like thirteen?"

"Fourteeeeeeeeen," Meredith answers.

"Fine, fourteen. Whatever. Don't you think you're a little too old to get tucked in?"

"No," Claire answers quickly.

I turn to Fantine hoping she'll confirm that my nighttime duties do not include bedtime stories, but she's too busy dealing with her own campers to offer me any help.

"Ugh, fine," I say. "I'll do it, just stop talking about it." Not like I'll be around to do it again.

"Yay!" Claire shouts and pumps her fist in the air. "Chirp! Chirp! Cricket's putting us to bed. Cricket's putting us to bed!"

Before I can say, "chirp again and die," the commotion of movie night starts up all over again. Meredith is popping wheelies in the dirt, yelling, "Cricket is the bedtime queeeeeen!" while Robyn, who made a miraculous recovery thanks to a bottle of Pepto, suddenly joins the festivities and is clapping her hands together, cackling like a hyena.

"Hey, what's going on over there?" Quinn's voice suddenly emerges from the other side of the dwindling campfire. "Are you trying to wake the dead?"

"Cricket's putting us to bed!" Claire calls back.

Mortified, I raise my head and glance in Quinn's direction.

Even through the hazy smoke, his gaze is penetrating. It momentarily makes me wonder if staying here would really be that bad.

"Awesome!" he calls back. "But you should probably start settling down. It's lights out in ten minutes. You need your beauty rest!"

"You're right, Quinn," I holler back. "We don't all have the natural beauty of a movie star!"

He lets out a hearty laugh. "Touché, Cricket," he says, before leaving to catch up with his own campers.

"I think he's hotter than Zac Efron," Claire says wistfully.

I can't help but laugh. "Yeah, he's pretty easy on the eyes."

"But he's no Edward Cullen, right?"

I'm not sure at what point in this ridiculous conversation Claire thought I invited her to touch me, but I feel her pudgy fingers wrap around my hand. "No, Claire," I say. "He's definitely no Edward Cullen."

✳ ✳ ✳

The beater pickup complete with the CAMP I CAN logo and blue handicapped tag swaying from the rearview wouldn't have been my first (or second) choice for my night on the town, but considering what my life has evolved into the last two days, I guess it shouldn't surprise me.

Quinn settles into the front seat with Colin, hardly noticing how amazing my butt looks in my skinny sevens, so I hop in the back next to Fantine, where we talk reality TV. I do my best to stay engaged in the conversation, but it's not easy. I'm way too focused on the night's future activities to focus on anyone from the Jersey Shore. It's when we pull into the stark parking lot of Ten Pin Lanes that my excitement begins to fade.

The building consists of little more than four crumbling walls, a tin roof, and a bum passed out between the Dumpster and chain-link fence. There are Coors Light signs hanging in the front windows, while a handwritten sign saying SHOES CLEANED MONTHLY is tacked to the front door.

"Is it even safe to go in there?"

"Don't worry, princess, we won't let anybody give you a tattoo," Fantine says, rolling her eyes. "Just think of it as an adventure."

An adventure. Right.

Collin finds a space near the back of the lot. The faint smell of cigarettes and concession food forces me to roll up my window before we actually stop. I'm the last to climb out of the truck, and when I do, I immediately link my arm through Quinn's. Under normal circumstances I'd never make the first move, but nothing about this circumstance is normal.

Quinn seems unfazed by my boldness. "I'm sure they're harmless," he says under his breath, referring to a couple of guys monitoring us from the back of a neighboring pickup. With their award-winning mullets and ability to throw back whiskey shots while still tongue-wrestling their chewing tobacco, I can see why he thought they were the cause of my angst. "And even if they do start something, we'll be fine. We know karate."

"We do?"

He nods. "We've seen *Karate Kid*, remember?"

I'm in the mood to get shit-faced and fired, not have a good time. But once again, Quinn's easy attitude gets the better of me and I begin to laugh.

We make our way across the broken asphalt, through the battered front doors, and straight into a white trash Wonderland. Flannel shirts, mullets, and cigarette butts, oh my!

I'm pleased to see that Colin heads straight to the bar, leaving the rest of us to search for a place to sit.

"How about this one," Fantine says, pointing to a plastic booth directly across the stained carpet from the shoe rental counter. Considering every surface in this place probably carries an infectious disease, I don't see the point in protesting.

I slide into the side of the booth opposite of Fantine. Quinn slides in beside me, his arm extending the length of the plastic cushion behind me.

"I'm guessing you don't do a whole lot of bowling," he says to me with a teasing grin.

"Something like that," I say.

"What is your typical Saturday night, Cricket?"

I look across the table and am surprised to see Fantine staring at me with a deadpan, Oprah-interviewing expression on her face.

"I don't know, just typical stuff I guess. Movies, shopping, parties."

"And who do you do these things with?"

"My friends," I say cautiously. "Why?"

"You mean you don't go with your boyfriend?"

"Uh, no." I pretend not to notice that Quinn's gaze has shifted from me to the faux wood grain of the tabletop. "I don't have a boyfriend."

"Are you kidding me?" Fantine smacks the table dramatically. "How could *you* not have a boyfriend? With all that blonde hair and a tan the Coppertone girls would kill for, that's just a shame. Wouldn't you agree, Quinn?"

My cheeks are ready to spontaneously combust. I'm not sure what sounds more appealing, hearing Quinn's answer or leaping across the table and pounding Fantine's head with my fists. Thank God Colin shows up.

"So what did I miss?" he asks, setting an ice-filled bucket of beers on the table. I waste no time grabbing one and taking a long pull. "Whoa, pace yourself, girl," he says. "You only get one."

What? How am I supposed to get drunk on one freaking beer?

"We were just prying into Cricket's life," Fantine says, answering Colin.

"Oh, then my timing's perfect." His eyes widen with curiosity as he takes a pull off his bottle. "I've been wondering about your name, Cricket."

"I'm sorry, what?" My brain is too busy reeling from this disappointing new development to properly keep up.

"Well, I'm guessing Cricket isn't your birth name?"

"Oh right. No, it's not. Cricket's been my nickname since I was a kid. My full name is Constance."

"You don't hear that one every day," Quinn says.

Nodding in agreement, I down another mouthful of beer as I try to come up with a solution to my limited beer supply while still staying engaged in the conversation. "Nobody ever calls me that anymore," I say. "Except when I'm in trouble."

"I hear that," Fantine adds. "I thought once I left for college my mom would relax a little, but she's even worse now. I can be upstairs in my room studying and she'll still be like, 'Carmen Fantena Galindo Marquez, you better not be doing what I think you're doing!' I swear, she just likes hearing the sound of her own voice." The whole table breaks into laughter, including me.

"Exactly," I say. "My dad practically rattles the windows when he yells at me with 'Constance Elaine Montgomery!'" I pause to take another drink, expecting to hear everyone laugh. Instead, there's just the distant sound of balls crashing into wooden pins. "What?" I say, as I look from one astonished face to another.

"Did you say your name was Constance Elaine Montgomery?" Colin asks.

"Yeah . . ."

"Montgomery?" Fantine adds.

"Yeah, what's the big deal?"

"Your dad is Lambert Montgomery?" Quinn takes a turn. "The real estate developer?"

"God, *yes*! What is wrong with you guys?"

They all exchange a hard glance before Colin falls back against the plastic seat. "I had no idea we were in the company of such greatness."

I feel my forehead crinkle the way it does when I'm working out a calculus problem. "What are you talking about?"

"Your dad signs our paychecks."

"What?" I laugh, though I'm not sure it's funny.

"It's true," Fantine says. "Your dad, or Montgomery Enterprises, has been keeping Camp I Can alive for the last thirteen years. Rainbow said they were about to go bankrupt, but a generous benefactor stepped in and saved it."

A seed of anxiety begins to take root in my gut. Dad knows about this place? He . . . saved it? Why would he do that? "And what makes you think this benefactor is my dad?"

"Besides the whole name on the bottom of our check thing, there's the plaque hanging in the office that says a substantial charitable contribution was made to the camp in memory of Constance Elaine Taft Montgomery," Fantine says and leans back, crossing her arms over her chest.

"Your dad didn't tell you about it?" Quinn asks.

I shake my head.

"He didn't say anything?"

Quinn's sympathetic tone is bad enough, but I can't help but feel a twinge of that same defensiveness I felt yesterday with Rainbow. Until I got here, I've never had to justify the inner-workings of mine and Dad's relationship to anyone. The people in my world just know how it works. Or they're smart enough not to ask.

"No, he didn't," I say. "But that doesn't mean anything. He donates to charities in my mom's honor all the time. It's good for taxes. And when you make as much money as he does, the IRS is always up your butt looking for ways to nail you on something."

I suck back the rest of my beer, wishing I had another to replace it with. Handicapped hell is one thing, but unloading the details of my jacked-up family is something entirely different.

"What happened to your mom, Cricket?" Fantine asks in a tone that's meant to be gentle but instead comes across as nosy.

"She died."

"Well, obviously. Was there an accident? Or was she sick or something?"

My chest tightens beneath her barrage of personal questions. Again, people in my world don't ask me these things because they already know the answers. They know how she died. They know my dad can't get over it. And they know we don't talk about her—ever.

I'm about to tell her to mind her own damn business, when I see one of the parking lot mullet brothers stagger through the front door and an idea pops into my head. "Yes, she was sick," I answer quickly. "She had breast cancer and died when I was four. Is that all you want to know, 'cause I really need to go to the bathroom."

Looking confused by the sudden turn in conversation, she says, "Yeah, that's all I wanted to know."

Quinn barely has enough time to exit the table before I'm crawling across the torn plastic seat and heading toward the bathroom.

"Do you want me to come with you?" Fantine calls after me.

"No," I say, not bothering to turn around. "I'm good."

Aware that they're probably watching me, I make a hard left at the hallway marked with a CRAPPER THIS WAY sign, but freeze as soon I round the corner and am out of sight. I do a quick ten count before looking back around the corner. As hoped, my tablemates have resumed their conversation and are fixated on each other rather than me.

Here goes nothing.

With my head down, I quickly cut back through the main entry area and out the front doors. The night air is thick and makes my lungs feel heavy. Already I long to be back inside where it's cooler, but turning around now isn't an option. Not when there's Jack Daniel's out here and I *have* to get drunk in order to earn a get-out-of-handicapped-jail free card.

Thanks to the fluorescent streetlamp mounted in the corner of the parking lot, I have more than enough light to see where I'm going. Not that I'd need directions to Red Neck Avenue. I sprint toward the entrance of the lot, more than surprising the mullet guy who is still camped out in the back of his truck.

"Hi. Um, I need . . . some of your Jack," I say, feeling like the world's biggest loser.

He stares at me with his mouth gaping. Leaning forward in his lawn chair, he says, "You what now?"

"I need a few shots of your Jack." I point to the bottle at his feet. "Please? I'm sort of . . . desperate."

I have no doubt he wasn't prepared for what I was going to say, but it's almost as if I'm speaking a foreign language. This dude is either too drunk to follow what I'm saying or he graduated from Camp I Can last year and just doesn't get it. "Look," I say, fishing a ten-dollar bill out of my pocket. "I'm going to take a couple of drinks from your bottle and then I'm going to give you this money, okay?" I extend my hand, offering him the cash.

His impaired gaze drifts from me to my hand and back to me again.

"Okay?" I repeat.

His response isn't immediate, and only comes after he hocks a chunk of tobacco over the side of his truck. "Help yerself," he says, nudging the bottle toward me with his foot. "And keep your cash."

NINE

"Y ou arrre really pretty. Have you ever cosiddered modeling?"

Through blurry eyes I see two identical versions of Fantine. All four of her eyes are rolling at me.

"Girl, you are messed up."

I snort. "Isn't it *awesome*!" I have no idea how much of that Jack I drank, but damn. I'm so rocked right now.

"How is it even possible that one beer can do that to someone?" Quinn asks.

"You got me," Fantine says.

"She's probably still dehydrated from yesterday," Colin says. "But it doesn't matter. This is going to be a huge problem for us."

"Whad'r you guys talkin' about?" I slap my hand against the table and do my best to stare them straight in their eyes. Which is proving to be a challenge. "I'm not a prob"—hiccup—"broblem. Yoooo on the other hand are a biiig problem, Mister!"

I look down to see that my hand has found its way to Quinn's chest, and my left leg is draped over his right thigh. *Ooopsy!* When did that happen?

"We gotta sober her up," Quinn says, easing my leg off of his.

"If Rainbow catches her like this, we'll all get fired."

I start laughing. It's just so ridiculous that I'm at this piece of crap bowling alley with Zac Efron. "Canihave"—hiccup—"your augotraph . . . aaauutograph, Mister Efffffron?"

"Shut up, Cricket," he says. "We're trying to figure something out."

I get serious, and prop my elbows up on the table. "So whadar we disss"—hiccup—"cussing?"

"Your drunk ass," Fantine says all bitchy.

"My ass?" I lean to the side and give my butt a smack. "It doesnint look drunk ta me. But it looks damn goooood in these jeans."

"I just might kill her," Fantine says.

"Whoa! Whoawhoawhoawhoa, whoa." I stare at her. Them. "Now you lisssen here. I . . . oh, God . . ."

"What's wrong with you?" she says.

"I don't . . . feel so good."

"Oh hell. Are you gonna puke?"

Both Fantines are blurry now, and there's a bad taste welling up in my throat. This is bad. "I . . . oh God. I think so. Yeah"—hiccup—"I need thuh bathroom. Now."

✳ ✳ ✳

"That sucks about her dad."

"Sounds like a jerk."

"Maybe that's why she's such a bitch. Daddy issues . . ."

As much as I try, I can only make out bits and pieces of the conversation going on around me. Everything is jumbled, like my brain is in a blender. My skin feels cold and clammy and my throat burns every time I swallow. "Coldplay blows," I mumble hoarsely. At least I think that's me.

"What'd she say?" comes a voice from the front seat.

"I thought she was asleep," says another voice.

"She's out of it, but I think it had something to do with Fantine's sucky DJ skills."

"Up yours, pretty boy."

The radio clicks off, and for a moment everything seems okay. I try to open my eyes, but the world starts spinning again. "What happened . . ."

"Ssshh." A warm hand touches my cheek, before settling into a divine rhythm of stroking my hair behind my ear. "Just close your eyes and go to sleep. You'll feel better in the morning."

"But . . ."

"It's okay. Just go to sleep, Cricket."

My eyes flutter open and for a moment I see the most beautiful pools of blue staring down at me. If I weren't so out of it, I'd totally jump in. "Okay," I say. And my eyes close.

TEN

"Rise and shine, Sleeping Beauty."

I try to open my eyes, but I'm pretty sure someone has glued them shut. "What do you want?" I grumble. "What's going on?"

"It's time for lunch. You gotta get up."

"Why are you yelling at me?"

I hear Fantine chuckle under her breath as the foot of my bed sags beneath her weight. "Cricket, do you remember anything about last night?"

Last night. Last night . . . Hillbillies, mullets, whiskey . . . "Oh God." I slowly pry my eyes open, and am greeted by a blurry Fantine and a pain in my head like nothing I've ever felt. "Last night was bad," I say, wincing at the ache in my throat.

"Yes, it was. It was kind of funny, too. But probably not for you."

I try to glare at her but that makes my face hurt, so I just close my eyes again and say, "Screw you."

"You wish. Now sit up, I brought you some Motrin."

"I don't think I can," I say. My tongue feels like sandpaper as it scrapes against the roof of my mouth. "I don't think I can ever sit up again. I'm going to die right here."

"Well, you don't have much choice. Haven't you ever had a hangover?"

"Not like this. I feel like crap."

"Which is pretty much how you look."

"I hate you so much right now," I say, doing my best to glare at her.

I hear her snort. "Likewise."

I sip from the plastic cup she's now holding in front of me and take the pills she drops in my hand. It's the best water I've ever tasted. "Give me more," I say, when the pills are safely down my throat. "Please, I'm so thirsty."

"Just chill. You'll start puking again if you drink too much right away."

"Again?"

"Uh, yeah. You threw up last night. Don't you remember?"

"Vaguely," I say, flopping my head back against the pillow.

"What'd you eat, anyway? I've never seen hot pink puke before. It was all over the bathroom."

I shake my head slowly, regretting last night's brilliant decision to cover up the whiskey smell with a handful of peppermints.

"I know it sucks," she says, "but it's actually a good thing you threw up. It saved our asses."

"What are you talking about?"

"Rainbow. We told her you must've had a bad reaction to the shrimp like Robyn did and that's why you were so out of it when we got home last night. Had she known you were trashed, we'd all have gotten busted and you'd be back in Chicago by now."

Chicago. Home.

Oh God . . . *No!*

I try and sit up, as if sudden movements will rewind time and I can have a do-over on my attempted escape, but the world is spinning way too fast for me to keep up. Instead, I collapse back against my pillow, ready to cry.

"Ah shit," she says, her voice taking on a slightly softer tone. "I was hoping you weren't still upset about it."

"About what exactly?"

She holds my gaze for a moment before heaving a deep breath. "I know why you took off for the bathroom last night."

"You do?" I ask nervously.

"It's all my fault. I never should have nagged you about your mom. You obviously didn't want to talk about it and . . . well, I'm sorry."

If my face wasn't already drained of its color, it would be now. "Uh . . . it's okay," I say, trying to quickly piece together a response. "I know you were just . . . curious because of my dad and the camp and everything. But it's fine. Really, I'm good now."

"Yeah?"

I nod. "Yeah. I'm fine."

"Well, good," she says. And by the sudden upturn in her voice I can tell that her relief is genuine. She stands up and looks down at me. "I know you don't wanna hear this right now, but Robyn recovered from her food poisoning in a matter of hours, which means your excuse has officially expired. You've got about twenty minutes until lunch, so I suggest you get yourself cleaned up and down to the mess hall before Rainbow starts getting suspicious."

I may hate the idea of this newly hatched plan, but I'm not about to throw Fantine and the boys under the bus because I can't hold my liquor.

"Okay," I say. "I'll get it together."

With a nod of approval, she disappears through the tiny doorway and I'm left alone to wallow in the steaming turd pile that has become my life.

"Idiot!" I scream into the safety of my faux down pillow.

All I had to do was drink enough to get kicked out, but instead I went completely Charlie Sheen and blew my one opportunity to get fired.

I pity-party for a solid five minutes before I determine that lying around smelling like a Porta-Potty isn't going to improve my situation. What I need is a new escape plan. And a shower.

✳ ✳ ✳

Somehow I manage to make it to the bathroom. I'm not sure how much time passes, but when I emerge my hair smells more of mangos than peppermint-laced puke. And thanks to a hearty tooth brushing, it no longer feels like a cat slept in my mouth. The one downside to cleaning up is that I have to change out of the T-shirt I woke up in. Which, if my fuzzy memory serves, was the same T-shirt Quinn wore when we went out last night. Swapping out my puked-on top for his clean one wasn't exactly how I envisioned our first clothes-free activity to go down, but at least chivalry isn't completely dead.

As I make my way through the camp grounds and toward the mess hall, my Cavalli lenses are about as effective as a piece of Saran wrap against the midday sun. How on earth am I going to get through an entire lunch without heaving? I pause at the bottom of the steps to catch my breath, when from the top of the stairs I hear, "How are you feeling today, Cricket?"

Squinting against the blinding sun, I look up to find Rainbow looking down at me. "Uh, okay I guess."

"Oh, thank goodness. I was worried. I had no idea you were allergic to shellfish."

I have an overwhelming urge to scream, *I'm not allergic to shellfish and why the hell would you know if I was?*—but I resist. Screaming feels like a whole lot of work right now.

"I guess we'll ask Sam to skip the lobster bisque he had planned for next week, huh? I don't want to run the risk of you and Robyn getting sick again." She laughs like she thinks she is funny, but I fail to see the humor. "We're having bean and cheese burritos today," she adds, her smile showing a hint of concern. "But I can ask Sam to make you something a little lighter. Maybe some toast or soup?"

"No," I say quickly. "A burrito actually sounds good." Like *freaking* good. "I'm sure that will be fine."

"Well, great. I think Claire saved you a seat—go help yourself."

I hobble my way up the remaining stairs, blowing by Rainbow with the most convincing smile I can muster, and stumble into the mess hall. My sudden need for grease overrides my irritation with life. I hardly flinch when I see Claire waving me down like an airliner.

"Chirp! Chirp!" she says. I take the empty seat between her and a boy who is wearing a duck-shaped oven mitt on his hand. "Do you like Mexican food? I love Mexican food!"

"I do today." Wasting no time digging into the basket of tortilla chips and bowl of salsa sitting in the center of the table.

"You smell like candy," says Oven Mitt.

"Good to know," I say, stuffing another salsa-drenched chip into my mouth.

I quickly polish off the entire basket of chips before I notice Quinn looking at me from the next table over.

"Hungry?" he says.

My initial instinct is to flee, but as my headache eases with each gram of sodium that enters my blood stream, I realize there's no point in being embarrassed. If puking on myself didn't turn him off, going Miss Piggy probably won't, either.

87

"You have no idea," I answer back.

The rest of lunch carries on in about the same fashion as it has every day since I've been here. Claire rambles on to no one in particular about the *American Idol* concert she's going to next month, and Meredith is using her fork as a microphone to perform Pink songs while Oven Mitt plays the drums with his spoon. I continue to stuff my face with more food than that Kardashian chick did during her pregnancy. All in all, I'm doing pretty well considering how my day started.

"Remind me what's on the agenda today," I say to Fantine as we escort our small herd from the mess hall back to the bunkhouses.

"We're hitting the pool for a few hours, then it's free time till dinner," she says.

"Really, the pool?" I'm feeling better with nine pounds of lard and a handful of Motrin in my gut, but baking under the sun doesn't sound particularly appealing. "Um . . . I think I might have just developed an allergy to Mexican food."

She laughs before flicking my arm with her finger. "Nice try, Miss Pukes-A-Lot, but your ass is officially healthy now and you *will* be at that pool."

On instinct, my bottom lip rolls out into a pout, but I don't say anything. With Fantine as my audience, I know there's no point.

* * *

"Damn, girl," Fantine says while surveying my skimpy hot pink bikini that Cambodian children probably slaved over. "If Quinn doesn't fall over dead when he sees you in that, then we know he's gay."

I think this is a compliment, but considering she's standing in front of me with washboard abs and looking like a model in her gold bikini, I can't help but feel a tad insecure. At least my food baby is gone. "I probably should've brought a one-piece," I say, tugging down on my top. "I had no idea camp would be, well, you know. It's probably not appropriate."

"Are you kidding me? Wait until you see what they're wearing."

She crosses the tiny space that makes up our bedroom and slides the curtain away from the wall. What she reveals is so shocking I have to blink hard to make sure I'm not hallucinating. Each of the five girls is sporting a bikini made of increasingly less fabric than the one standing beside it.

"Whoa. I never would have thought they'd be into making that big of a statement at the pool." No matter how horrible a statement it might be.

"Oh, they are. They're all about turning heads and getting attention. They might be different than us on the outside, but they're really just normal teenage girls, too."

I'm not sure what I consider these girls to be, but *normal* has never crossed my mind.

"All right, ladies," Fantine says, striding into the main cabin area. "Let's hit the pool!"

"Do you work out a lot or something?" I ask Fantine. "Nothing on your body moves or shakes at all."

"I guess that's what training for four hours a day will get you," she says with a smirk. "Big muscles, ripped abs, and a tight ass." She pats herself on the backside and generates a round of applause from some of the girls.

"What kind of training do you do?" I ask.

"Sheeeeeeeee's a sprinter!" Meredith says proudly, rolling between us and wearing a smile almost as bright as her orange bikini. "Sheeeee's going to the Olympics!"

"Well, one of us is," says Fantine, high-fiving her two-wheeled friend.

"Wait . . . what? You're going to the Olympics? Like *the* Olympics?"

"I wish." Fantine laughs. "The Olympics were my lifetime dream, but once I got a taste of college-level competition last year, it proved to be enough for me. This one, on the other hand, has already been to the Olympics and won a silver medal. Isn't that right, Meredith?"

"You did?" I make no attempt to hide my shock.

"That was laaaast year. Next yeeeear I'm getting the goooooold!"

"Damn straight you are," Fantine says.

I find myself nodding with an artificial smile, as I try to make sense of what I've just heard. At nineteen Fantine has already pursued a lifetime dream. The only lifetime dream I have involves me and a limit-free Visa. But the real mind-number is that Hannah Montana and her wheelchair of doom has made it to the freaking Olympics. How is that even possible?

Before I have time to rationalize the absurdity of what I've just heard, my arms are loaded down with sunscreen and flotation devices, and I'm in the middle of a handicapped procession toward the swimming pool. Claire is on my right blathering on about some kid named James she can't wait to play Marco Polo with, and Meredith is rolling along on my left, whistling a tune I recognize from *The Sound of Music*. Ordinarily I'm not a big fan of whistling, but today it's kind of soothing. I'm probably still drunk.

When we arrive at the swimming pool, I quickly determine that it is far from the infinity-edge country club pool I'm used to. There are no waterfalls, no lounge chairs with WiFi/Bluetooth capability, and no bubbly waitstaff eager to bring me a lemonade. Instead, I get a rectangular-shaped hole in the ground with stairs at one end and a thousand-foot-long wheelchair ramp at the other. The glamour factor is staggering.

"What took you guys so long?" Quinn yells from the far end of the pool. As subtly as possible, I glance in his direction for my first sober glimpse of shirtless Quinn. Damn . . .

"Duuuh! Weee had to get beauuuuuuutiful," Meredith answers in her most dramatic voice. With catlike dexterity, she manages to steer herself with one hand while simultaneously releasing her hair from its pigtailed prison with the other. Her long red tresses fall easily over her shoulders, and she runs the fingers of her free hand through them very slowly, proving she's got a lot more game than I ever would have imagined.

"I told you they meant business," Fantine says, giving her own tail feathers a dramatic shake while I surprise myself and actually laugh out loud.

"Well, you did a good job," Quinn says behind squinted eyes. "Isn't that right, guys?"

"Agreed!" Colin calls from the opposite end of the pool. A few pathetic whistlers chime in while Oven Mitt offers up his best catcall.

The girls giggle at the attention, and I find myself smiling—forgetting for a brief moment that these people are not actually my friends.

"Why are they such pathetic creatures?" Fantine says under her breath.

I peer over my lenses and see that every male eye in the pool, even the googly one that's usually looking elsewhere, is trained on us.

"Boys are silly sometimes," Claire says behind a schoolgirl grin. Without a shred of modesty, she steps out of her tent-size cover-up and presents herself in full, barely covered glory. From behind the safety of my glasses, I wince as her gleaming white butt cleavage makes its debut around the thin strip of neon fabric. Much to my surprise, no one laughs or makes jokes at this nightmarish display. Instead, there's just one stuttering voice rising up from the back of the pool.

"C-C-Claire! Are y-you ready to p-p-play?"

"Yes!" she screams, thundering her way across the cement. "I'm coming for you, James!"

Ah-ha. James—aka Oven Mitt.

Claire plunges into the pool with the grace of a hippo, while I'm left to wonder what sort of alternate universe I'm living in. Girls with no legs win Olympic medals and girls whose asses have just eaten their own bathing suits aren't made fun of.

"Coooome on, Cricket!" Meredith calls from the pool's edge. She's dragging her hands through the water while her legs dangle in the water below her. "The waaaaater is great!"

"Uh, yeah. Okay." I shimmy off my cutoffs, and am just pulling my tank top over my head, when I see Meredith face-plant into the water. "Oh my God! Is she okay?"

Without waiting for an answer, I race toward the pool's edge, prepared to jump in after her.

"Cricket, wait!" Fantine's instruction grabs my attention only a moment before I feel her death grip on my arm.

"She's going to drown!" I say, trying to wiggle away from her.

"No, she's not," Fantine says, in a voice that seems much too calm given the circumstances. "Look at her." With her free hand, she points toward the deep end of the pool where two pale arms are cutting through the water.

I blink hard to make sure I'm not seeing things. "Holy crap."

"Pretty amazing, huh?"

Amazing is David Beckham in an underwear ad. This is something entirely different.

"Yeah," I say, my head shaking in disbelief. "It's . . . wow. I had no idea you could swim without, uh . . ."

"Legs?"

I look down to find Quinn staring up at me. His tanned arms are crossed on the lip of the pool, and the smile on his face is radiant.

"Yeah," I admit with a shrug. "That's probably really stupid of me, huh?"

"Nah," he says, and now it seems his eyes are smiling, too. "Most people probably can't swim without the use of their legs. But Meredith is pretty exceptional. Most swimmers at her level have some use of their legs, but not her—all her power comes from her arms. She's got some serious guns to contend with. I'm pretty sure she could take me."

"Somehow I doubt that," I say, admiring the beads of cool water glistening on his firm shoulders and perfectly defined biceps. Zac Efron has nothing on Quinn in the muscle department.

"So what about you, do you swim?"

"Well, I *can*," I say, tossing my tank to the ground. "But I don't do it competitively or anything." Like I do anything competitively.

"I guess I'm not much of an athlete. What about you?" Although he's subtle, I still catch him taking a glimpse at my bikini. I can't help but smile. Claire is right, boys are silly sometimes. "What about you?" I ask again.

"Huh? Oh yeah," he says. "I . . . play soccer."

"Soccer. That's right. Fantine told me about the scholarship. That's awesome."

"It's only a partial, but it helps. Without it there's no way my parents could afford to send me there."

I think back to the T-shirt I woke up in. My heart starts beating a little faster. "DePaul, right?"

He nods. "It's got a solid engineering program and it's not too far away, so it worked out well."

"So that's what you want to do then? Be an engineer?"

"Something along those lines," he says. "I've always liked piecing things together—constructing things and stuff. There are a lot of different fields I can get into with an engineering degree, so I figured it was a good fit. What about you? What are your plans after graduation next year?"

His question catches me by surprise. Not because I haven't been asked about it before, but because for the first time I feel like I should know the answer. Or might actually want to know the answer.

"I'm still debating," I lie. "I have a couple different things in mind but I'm not ready to say anything for sure."

"Holding out for a big announcement, huh?"

"Yeah," I say. Or a revelation.

"Do I even get a hint?"

I stare down at the cute little wrinkle that has suddenly formed in the center of his forehead, and wish I could. Other than trying to land that striped Burberry bag I spied last month, I haven't given much consideration to my future at all.

"Nope," I say, shrugging off my insecurities with a smirk. "You'll have to wait like everybody else."

"You're no fun," he says, and splashes my legs with water. "Well, I'm sure whatever it is it'll be great. I can't wait to hear what it is."

"Yeah," I say.

You and me both.

ELEVEN

Somewhere in Katie's magazine vault, there's an article detailing how stupid it is for girls to go starry-eyed over a guy they've just met. Before Quinn, I'd have nominated that author for some sort of magazine award. Now, I'm pretty sure I'd be the inspiration for the story.

In my head, I am aware that my infatuation for Quinn could be considered embarrassing. But try as I might, I can't convince my heart and my body to respond any differently than they are. Besides the gorgeous, makes-my-insides-turn-to-Jell-O factor, he's also sweet, funny, and painfully smart. Which is why I nearly strip off my pajamas and offer myself to him on a bed of poison oak when he shows up outside my window with a flashlight and that cute, lop-sided grin.

"What do you want, Pretty Boy?" Fantine says through the dusty window screen. "Aren't you the one always telling us we need our beauty sleep?"

"I'm not here for you, Marquez," he says from the shadows. "I want to borrow Cricket for a few minutes."

We are already sharing what limited space our tiny window

frame allows, but as soon as I hear Quinn's request, I shove her out of the way and press my forehead against the screen. "Hey, Quinn. What's up?"

Fantine falls back against her bed, laughing at my lack of subtlety while I shush her with my hand.

"Can you come out for a few minutes?"

"Yeah! Just give me a sec." I hop off my bed and begin the mad search for my flip-flops.

"You are officially pathetic. You know that, right?"

"I'm not pathetic," I say, clawing through the dark for my damned left shoe. "I just want to see what he wants, that's all. Ah-ha!" I pull the flip-flop out from under the bed and give it a quick shake, praying no spiders have taken up residence. "I'm just a hospitable person."

"Hospitable? *You?* Just promise me you'll use a condom."

"Ew! You're disgusting," I say, tossing my pillow over her smirky face. "You're just jealous because Colin's not out there doing the same thing for you right now."

"Colin? Oh please. That boy wouldn't know what to do with a girl if you gave him an instruction manual. Besides, I don't date men under twenty-five. Or over seven feet."

"Whatever. You know you'd be all over him if he offered."

She snorts. "In his dreams."

"Okay, fine, I'm outta here. Don't wait up."

"Have fun," she says. "And remember, don't do anything I

wouldn't do."

Now it's my turn to snort. "Like that's even possible."

In an exaggerated attempt not to wake the girls, I creep through the main cabin and slide out onto the front porch. Quinn is waiting for me on the bottom step. He looks so dreamy beneath the silvery moonlight that I have to grab the handrail so I don't fall over.

"What's up?" I say, sounding a lot calmer than I actually am.

"Hey, I wanted to talk to you about something. I was hoping for a little privacy."

"Uh . . . yeah. Sure." Not exactly the do-you-wanna-taste-my-ChapStick invitation I was hoping for, but it'll do.

I fall in line beside him as we head up the paved trail that leads away from the cabin. The air feels extra muggy tonight and, per usual, the mosquitoes are in full grazing mode. But much like wheelchairs and lazy eyes, when Quinn's nearby they don't seem to bother me as much.

"Where exactly are we going?" I ask, realizing that my flip-flops don't make the best hiking shoes.

"It's a surprise."

"But you do know where you're going, right? We're not just wandering for the sake of wandering. . . ."

He stops suddenly, turning his head over his shoulder to look at me. "Why, Miss Montgomery, you're not scared of the dark, are you?"

"No, Mr. Youngsma," I say, with an equal amount of sarcasm. "I'm not scared of the dark. I'm scared of tripping and adding another Band-Aid to my collection."

Despite the darkness I see him smile. "Well, you have a point there. I'm pretty sure Pete's all out of vampires, which means you'd probably be stuck with SpongeBob, so . . . here." He extends his hand toward me. "I should probably help you the rest of the way."

"Such a gentleman." I drop my hand into his and nearly melt. It's as warm as I remember. I clutch that hand until we finally descend down a steep, overgrown hill and into a leaf-carpeted gully and he releases me.

"So what do you think?" he says, aiming his tiny flashlight in front of us. "Was it worth the hike?"

The dim beam can't possibly enhance the view the moonlight already provides. "Wow," I say, stepping forward to survey one of the gray, ancient-looking trees. I graze my hand along its trunk. The way the roots erupt through the ground reminds me of Carolyn's fingers, all bent and knobby. "This is so cool. It's like something out of a *Harry Potter* movie. I feel like the trees are going to start talking or something."

"I know, isn't it awesome? I stumbled across it last summer." Like some sort of pretty-boy ninja, he begins hopping and leaping his way through the maze of bending roots. "I come out here some- times when I feel like I need a break from things at camp," he says, balancing a foot on a particularly narrow root. "It can get a little intense sometimes."

"Intense is a bit of an understatement," I say, watching him cautiously.

"Yeah, maybe sometimes. But you seem to be handling it pretty well, now that you've recovered from your world-class hangover, that is."

"Okay, there it is," I say with a groan. "You've been waiting all day to say that, haven't you?"

"To say what?" he says playfully.

"To tell me I'm a shitty drunk."

Beneath the rays of intermittent moonlight I see him grin. "You're a shitty drunk."

"I know," I say, burying my face in my hands. "I have no idea what happened. One minute I'm fine and the next . . ."

"Don't remind me," he says. "I'm trying to erase the memory from my mind as we speak. I'm still not sure how you pulled that off, though. I've never seen one beer mess somebody up that bad. I guess it's safe to assume you don't drink very often, huh?"

"Oh no," I say. "I drink all the time at home." He crosses his arms over his chest, raising a skeptical brow. "Okay, maybe I don't drink *that* often . . . but still, I don't know how that could have happened. It must be all this fresh air getting to me. Don't forget, I'm a city girl."

"Oh, I don't think I'll ever be able to forget that." He motions toward my *Twilight*-covered knee. "But that's actually sort of what I wanted to talk to you about."

"My inability to hold booze?"

"Well, no. Although we'll probably have to work on that in the future. I wanted to talk to you about your life back in Chicago—your dad, to be more specific."

"My dad?"

"Yeah. When we told you about your dad's involvement with the camp you seemed a little . . ."

"Annoyed? Yeah, that's 'cause I already told you guys, he's involved with tons of charities. It's really not a big deal that he didn't tell me about this one."

"Okay, okay"—he steps forward, one hand raised in defense—"I'm not trying to get you all worked up. What your dad does or doesn't tell you is none of my business, or anyone else's—"

"You know, Quinn, if you wanted to talk to me about my dad's business arrangements, you didn't have to drag me out here in the middle of the night. You could've just asked me at breakfast."

"No," he says, running a hand through his hair. "That's not why I brought you out here. That's not what I meant to say."

"Then why am I here?"

"I don't know." He looks flustered. "I guess I wanted to tell you that it doesn't matter to me that your dad is the person who signs my paychecks." Recognizing the confusion on my face, he immediately adds, "Last night you said you've been burned by people who just want to hang out with you 'cause you're rich."

Damn, drunk mouth!

"I just want you to know that I'm not one of those people. Whether your dad has money or not won't change the way I feel about you."

My eyes widen. "How you feel about me?"

"Yeah," he says, taking another step toward me. "I like you, not your money."

Considering how many people have liked me for the wrong reasons, Quinn's sweet confession shouldn't be lost on me. But tonight it is. I can't focus on anything but those three little words he just said.

"You like me?"

The slight nod of his head is enough to answer my question, but it's the grin breaking across his face that sets my heart racing.

"I think that's pretty obvious, don't you?"

I shrug, still dumbfounded by the sudden turn of events.

"Well, I do." He takes another step closer. "A lot."

He's less than a foot away from me now, and despite the sudden lack of oxygen in my lungs, I manage to rattle off a question I can't believe I'm asking. "What exactly do you like about me?"

He seems amused, but still cocks his head as if he's carefully considering his response. "Well . . ." He shuffles forward, eliminating all the space that separates us. "I like that you say what's on your mind."

I swallow hard. "Yeah?"

He nods. "And the way you stress out about your makeup getting messed up at the pool." His gaze deviates momentarily to my mouth. "I like the way the dirty window screen imprint looks right here." He reaches forward and gently grazes my forehead with his thumb. "And how you looked in my T-shirt last night."

"I'm sorry about that," I manage to say. "I woke up this morning and had no idea what was going on, and then I saw your shirt. It took me a minute to figure out it was yours—"

"And I really like the way you babble when you're nervous."

Before I have the wherewithal to shut up on my own, I feel his lips cover mine and the taste of cinnamon floods my mouth.

I lace my fingers around his neck and pull him closer. He knots his hand in my hair, a confirmation that he's been wanting this as much as I have.

I lose myself in his touch, in the way his breath feels against my skin, and momentarily forget that my world outside his arms still contains handicapped signs and slurred speech. I could seriously stay here forever. Which is why when he asks, "Would you be willing to risk another trip out here again sometime?" I don't hesitate in my response.

"Definitely," I say, breathing a contented sigh. "Most definitely."

TWELVE

I am so screwed it's not even funny.

Up until the kiss I wanted nothing more than to escape this freak farm. But now everything is just so damned complicated.

The past two nights, Quinn and I have spent countless hours getting to know each other while the rest of Camp Kill Me Now snoozes in their rickety beds. Fantine is convinced that we're just rounding the bases beneath the trees, but believe it or not, our midnight adventures actually involve a lot more talking than kissing. Which is exactly why my dad's return four days from now is starting to stress me out.

If I follow through with my original plan, I run the risk of losing Quinn (which is exactly why I'm staying tight-lipped about my failed drunken escape). The flip side is that I'm not entirely confident his gentle lips are enough to see me through the duration of my sentence. And as much as I love spending time with him, I'm not sure I can hang with the heavy, handicapped price tag he comes with.

"Is everything okay? You're abnormally quiet tonight."

Wrapped in Quinn's arms beneath a sea of stars, and nearly a mile between me and the nearest wheelchair, I shouldn't have a care in the world. But I do—a big one. I quickly come up with an excuse for my atypical behavior. Much to my surprise, it's actually legitimate.

"I was just thinking about my dad. We've never gone this long without talking before."

"I'm sure he wants to talk to you," he says. "It's probably just the time difference or issues with his cell. They don't all work internationally, you know."

I nod because his efforts to console me are sweet, not because I agree with him. My dad has access to the best technology out there. If he wanted to get a hold of me, he could.

"You should take a trip up the hill tomorrow. Maybe the timing will work out and you'll catch him between meetings or something."

Truth is, I'd already planned to tackle cell phone hill after tomorrow afternoon's hike, but I wouldn't want Quinn to think I don't appreciate his advice.

"That's a good idea," I say. "Plus Carolyn's probably left me a message by now. It would be nice to hear her voice."

"Who's Carolyn?"

"She's our housekeeper," I say, feeling somewhat weird that our home lives haven't really come up yet. Not that I've minded. "And the closest thing I've ever had to a mom." Considering I've never said those words aloud, the conviction in my voice surprises me.

"Oh," he says, his expression softening. "Wow. I guess you two have been through a lot together then, huh?"

I nod. "She was the one who took care of my mom when she was sick. But of course I don't remember any of that."

He offers a sincere smile, before allowing his gaze to drift away from me and to the silhouettes of the moonlit trees surrounding us.

"I don't mean to sound like a jerk, but you're probably better off. Watching someone die isn't easy. Those memories will stay with you forever."

"You watched someone die?"

"My older brother," he says. "About four years ago."

My eyes fall shut. Losing a mom you never knew sucks, but losing a brother you shared memories with is just brutal.

"I'm so sorry, Quinn," I say, repositioning myself so I can nuzzle my head into that little corner of space between his chin and his chest. "Life is just so unfair sometimes."

I feel him nod against my head, but he doesn't actually speak again for a long time. And when he finally does, I'm surprised by his response. "You know what, I'm glad life is unfair sometimes."

"Huh? What are you talking about?"

"Well, think about it. If life was always fair, you never would have ended up coming here and then I never would have met you. In this case, I think the unfairness of life worked in my favor."

"Is that a line from some Efron movie I haven't seen?"

"Pfff, whatever," he says, waving away my question. "I don't need Efron to make me look good. I look good on my own, baby. I'm the smoothest-talking cat in town."

"Oh my God." I cover my face with my hands, embarrassed for him. "You did *not* just say that."

"Hell yeah, I did," he says, continuing with his goofy act. "Everybody's talking about it. They're like, 'There goes Quinn. He's so smooth, just look at him. Efron wishes he was half as cool as Quinn. . . .'"

My laughter cuts him off only seconds before his own.

"You're a freak," I say.

"Yeah, well, it takes one to know one," he says. "But actually, there must be some truth to my smooth-talking skills. Rainbow asked if I wanted to emcee the show. I told her I was in, but wanted to make sure you were cool with it first. Seeing how you're the boss and all."

Why did he have to derail our conversation by bringing *her* up?

"Uh-oh. What'd I say?"

"Nothing."

"Come on," he prods, jabbing a finger into that very ticklish spot just above my waist. "What's wrong? Did you want to emcee?"

"God no." I swat his hand away before he can tickle me again. "I'm just not that interested in talking about Rainbow, that's all."

"Why? Did something happen between you two?"

"If by something you mean, does she creep me out? Then yes."

The confused look on his face slowly gives way to one that

borders more on the side of amusement. "Rainbow creeps you out?"

"*Yes*," I say, very aware of the sarcasm in his voice.

"Like *American Horror Story* creepy or Nicki Minaj creepy?"

"*Quinn*," I say, smacking his chest. "I'm being serious."

"Okay, okay, I'm sorry. I promise I'll be serious. What does she do that creeps you out?"

"She stares at me."

His eyes narrow. "She . . . stares at you?"

"Yes, a lot. But it's not like she's just casually watching me; it's like she's observing me. Like she's taking mental notes about every little thing I do so she can write a book about me or something."

"Why would she want to write a book about you?"

"Because she thinks I'm a spoiled brat."

"*What?*"

Now I have his attention.

"It's true. She thinks I'm a spoiled brat. She told me herself."

"Are you serious? When?"

"The first day I was here. Right before I took off running up the hill, she told me I was an insolent, spoiled brat and that if I didn't get with the program I needed to leave."

He reels his head back. "That doesn't seem like something she'd say."

"Yeah, well, people aren't always what they seem."

Even though it's dark, I'm still able to recognize the disappointment on his face. It sucks to be the bearer of bad news. "No," he finally says. "I guess they're not."

We sit quietly for a moment, before he says, "Well, if it makes any difference, I don't think you're a brat."

"That's just because I let you kiss me."

"Well, there is that. But besides the obvious physical benefits of hanging out with you, I really don't think you're a brat."

"Thank you," I say, peeking over my shoulder at him. "But you didn't say I wasn't spoiled."

"Well, I think we both know that you've got it pretty good."

"Excuse me?" I whip my head over my shoulder and look him dead in the eye. "Whose side are you on?"

"Whoa. Yours, of course. But you didn't let me finish. I was going to say that being spoiled isn't your fault. Your dad has you living in a bubble, Crick. Private schools, personal drivers, ritzy vacations . . . Can't you see how someone might label that as being spoiled?"

On instinct, I open my mouth to retaliate against his words. But as they roll around in my head, I realize there might be some truth to them. I do sort of live in a bubble. A very posh, fancy bubble, but a bubble nonetheless.

"That still doesn't justify her calling you a brat, though," he continues, his voice carrying a cautious tone. "And now that she's gotten to know you, I'm sure her opinion's changed anyway."

"Why would her opinion have changed?"

"Because you're kicking ass with the kids. Now that she's seen you in action, there's no way she can still feel that way."

Kicking ass with the kids. . . . Oh, man. I am totally going to hell.

THIRTEEN

The next afternoon I claw my way up cell phone hill in search of a little Windy City pick-me-up. As I feared, my dad hasn't left any messages, but I am grateful to find a voice mail from Carolyn. Other than informing me that Mr. Katz has gone schizo and is barking at his own tail, there's nothing particularly informative about her call. I still manage to get a little choked up, though. Her accent never sounded so beautiful.

I'm halfway through the second play-through of the message, when the beeping in my ear alerts me that someone is calling me right now. I glance down at the screen and see Katie's picture pop up.

"Oh my God! Katie?"

"Cricket? Hello?"

"I can hardly hear you!" I shout into the phone, staggering around like a drunk in search of a stronger signal.

"Can you hear me now?" she says, finally coming in loud and clear.

"Yes. Thank God." I settle onto a large, moss-covered rock on the far side of the hill and heave a sigh of relief. It's so good to hear her voice. "Where are you?"

"I'm at the beach with some people I met a couple of days ago. There's this guy, Shane—oh my God, Crick, he's so hot and totally into me. I'm having so much fun!"

"That's great," I say, eager for my own turn at boy talk. "What's he like?"

"Not sure really. He's super cute and drives an H2. That's as far as we've gotten. So what's the deal there? Are the retards still driving you crazy?"

I hear a chorus of laughter in the background, and by the muffling sound against the phone, can tell Katie's joining in with them. I suddenly feel very alone.

"They're not completely retarded," I say. "They can actually feed themselves and even know how to use the toilet." She returns to our conversation with a hearty laugh. "Of course you still have to get over the whole smashed-in, dog-faced look, but I suppose life would be boring if we were all gorgeous and desirable."

"I suppose," she says, and in my mind I can see her dark eyes rolling. "I still can't believe your dad did this to you. I mean, what the hell? Sentencing you to work at a 'tard farm. That's so unfair. Have you talked to him yet?"

"No, but I'm not surprised. I told you he was really pissed. I'm sure I'll hear from him when he gets home in a few days."

"But you're surviving, right?"

"Yeah, it's definitely gotten better since the last time we talked."

"Oh my God, that's right! What's up with the hottie? Don't tell me you're swapping spit with some one-legged freak."

"He's got two legs," I say. "But yeah, he's totally hot. In fact, he looks just like Zac Efron if you can believe that."

"No shit? Shane and I just watched that cheesy Nicholas Sparks movie he was in. Totally predictable but he was still smokin'. So what's the deal? Is he loaded? What kind of car does he drive?"

"Uh . . ." I find myself stalling for time, as I grow surprisingly uncomfortable with her line of questioning. "He doesn't come from money, and he hasn't mentioned anything about a car. But he's super smart and really funn—"

"I'm coming!" She cuts me off to yell to someone in the background. "He sounds great, Crick, but I gotta run. Call me when you get home."

The call goes dead before I even have a chance to say good-bye, and I'm left to wonder whether or not Katie is actually the person I want to get a matching tattoo with next year.

"Cricket?"

I turn my head, transforming into my usual mess of giggles and warm, happy fuzzies when I discover Quinn standing just a few feet behind me.

"How do you always manage to sneak up on me?" I ask, rising to greet him. "I swear I must be going deaf. Is it dinnertime already?"

His distant look sends a chill down my spine.

"What's wrong?"

"Is that really what you think?"

"What?" I ask, walking slowly toward him. "What is it?"

"Who were you talking to?"

"Katie," I answer cautiously. "Why?"

"So what you were saying to her—that's really what you think?"

I think back to my brief and incredibly disappointing conversation with my best friend. Beach parties, retards, cars . . . Oh, he's wondering about what I said about him. "Of course I think those things," I say. "You *are* the smarte—"

"God, Cricket!" He silences me with a tone I've never heard him use before. On instinct I backpedal a few feet. "I'm not talking about me. I'm talking about what you said about *them*—about the campers. Is that really what you think of them?"

For the first time in my life, I'm absolutely speechless.

"Let me remind you," he says in that same biting tone. "Smashed-in, dog-faces who can actually use the toilet. Does that sound familiar?"

"Oh my God," I mutter. His eyes are overflowing with anger. It's all I can do not to cry. "Stop looking at me like that! Let me explain."

"What is there to explain?" He raises his hands in question. "You either feel that way or you don't. It's not that hard. Just answer the question."

Wide-eyed, I stare at him, praying that I don't burst into a ball of flames right here on the hilltop. Never in my life would I have imagined that one simple question could reduce me to feeling like the lowest form of life on the earth—but it just happened. And now Quinn is looking at me like he'd rather see me dead than hear my answer.

"I . . . it's just . . . I've never been around people like them before! I didn't mean anything by it. I was just BSing with Katie—"

"You don't get it, do you?" He rakes a shaky hand across his forehead. "You're so wrapped up in your own perfect world that you can't see you're doing to them exactly what you don't want people to do to you. What Rainbow did to you. You hated that she judged you for something you have no control over, but you're doing the same thing to them! They have as much control over the way they came into this world as you do."

The burning sensation in my throat nearly cripples me as I try again to step closer, only to be given a dismissive wave in return. "I don't know what you want me to say! What can I say to make you understand?"

"Understand? Are you kidding me? What could you possibly say that would help me understand what you just said?"

Again, no words.

"That's right, Cricket, because you can't. There's no way to justify that."

"Wait!" I beg as I see him start to walk away. "Please, Quinn. What about the last few days . . . and last night? Didn't that mean anything to you?"

"Don't even go there, Cricket," he shouts back, turning to face me with heat in his eyes. "Every minute I've put in with you has been real. Especially last night. I didn't make you believe I was somebody I wasn't, or that I cared about you when I didn't. You had me feeling sorry for you—had me believing that you actually cared what people thought of you. What *I* thought of you. But the truth is you don't give a shit what anybody thinks and you certainly don't care about anybody else."

His words hit me like a fist to the gut.

"Please just wait," I plead, reaching out to him as tears flow freely down my cheeks. He keeps his head down, refusing to look at me. "You're wrong," I say. "Everything I've ever said to you is real. I've shared more with you than anyone in my life. You have to believe me, Quinn."

He raises his head to look at me. His stare is cold and unfeeling.

"I can't believe I was so stupid. Here I thought that under all that makeup and privilege was this funny, beautiful person who the world made assumptions about without giving her a fair shake, but you're not. The Cricket I thought I knew would never have said things like that."

"I'm sorry," I sputter. "But it's not like I said those things about you!" *Oh God, stop babbling, you idiot!* "I'm so sorry, Quinn. I don't know why I said that. I just . . . I don't want you to think I'm some bitch—"

"Too late," he says, devoid of all emotion. "And for the record, I drive a '97 Chevy pickup. It's got a big ass dent in the bumper and the upholstery's torn to shreds. Make sure you tell Katie."

His contempt for me is tangible, and follows behind him like a wake as he disappears down the side of the hill. I collapse onto the ground and begin to weep. Never in my life has one person's opinion of me mattered so much. Or hurt so bad.

FOURTEEN

I heard you might be up here."

I silence the woe-is-me song I've been listening to for the last hour and turn toward the fading sun. Colin is standing in front of me, wearing a sympathetic grin that makes me want to start crying all over again.

"Everything okay?"

"Yeah . . . I'm fine. Just needed a little alone time."

"Okay." His ultrasmooth tone confirms he knows I'm full of crap. "Mind if I sit down for a minute?"

"Go ahead"—I shrug—"it's a free country."

He strides toward me, his long legs covering miles of distance in mere feet, and settles on the ground with his back against the rock I'm perched on. He closes his eyes and cradles his head in his hands, inhaling like he's just stumbled into a Starbucks on a blustery winter morning.

"Man, that fresh air is good. I think my lungs expand a foot every time I come up here. Going back to the city after a month out here is always a shock to my system."

"Where do you live?" I ask. Not because I really care, but

because a meaningless conversation will be a good distraction from thinking about Quinn.

"Chicago. Same as you."

"You do?"

"Yep. I grew up in Lincoln Park."

"*You* live in Lincoln Park?"

"Yeah." His head cocks slightly, offering me a glimpse of his gleaming white grin. "Is that so hard to believe?"

"No. I'm just . . . surprised that's all. We're practically neighbors."

"Yeah, I heard. The Gold Coast, huh?"

"Astor Street. Who told you where I live?"

"Rainbow. She mentioned it the other day when I asked her about your dad."

"Wait," I say, leaning forward so I can see his face. "You asked her about my dad? What'd she say?"

"I thought you didn't care about his affiliation with the camp."

"Colin . . ."

"I'm just messin' with you. She just said that she and your father go a long way back. She didn't offer up any other information, and I didn't really feel comfortable prying, so I let it go."

"They go a long way back? What the hell does that mean?"

"I don't know," he says. "You'll have to ask her yourself."

"Right," I mumble. "I'll be sure to do that."

A week ago, I would have been nervous sitting so close to an enormous black guy I hardly know, and with very little light left in the day, but not today. Colin is about as comfortable as a pair of old sweatpants, and the shared silence is exactly what I need after my rotten afternoon.

Several minutes pass before he asks, "Did Quinn tell you why he works here every summer?"

Besides life on the home front, camp life was the only other subject Quinn and I seemed to avoid. Mostly because when we were alone together, I tried to pretend it didn't exist. "Not specifically."

He nods his head, and I can't help but wonder what he's thinking. Probably the same horrible things Quinn does.

"It doesn't surprise me. He's really private about that part of his life. I probably shouldn't be the one to tell you this, but given the circumstances, I think you ought to know. Quinn's older brother, Ethan, was a camper here."

My jaw drops. "He was?"

"Yep, he had Down's syndrome. Just like Claire," he adds strictly for my benefit. "He died unexpectedly a few years ago—some complication with a surgical procedure, but while he was alive, Quinn was obviously really protective of him. He got into more fights defending him than he'd ever admit to. That's why he's hypersensitive to people making fun of handicapped kids—he's still in protective brother mode."

The intimate conversation Quinn and I shared last night

suddenly hits me on a much deeper level, and I seriously feel like I might throw up. "Crap," I say. No wonder he got so pissed. He was defending his brother—from me.

"So I guess he told you what happened between us?"

"Not in detail," he says, offering a smile more generous than I deserve. "But I know that for him to have said anything to me, he must be hurting pretty bad."

"Bad doesn't really cover it. He hates me."

"He doesn't hate you."

"Yes, he does."

"No. He's pissed at you, but it doesn't mean he's done with you. It just means you've got a lot of work to do to make it right. And that boy can hold a grudge, so be prepared."

"Be prepared? That's your advice?"

He shrugs.

"Well, that's *real* encouraging, Colin. Thank you so much."

"Aw, you'll be fine," he says. "You'll make it right."

"How can I possibly make this right? The last time I saw him he was ready to kill me with his bare hands."

He pushes himself off the rock and turns toward me so we meet eye to eye. "It's easy. You just do it."

I wait patiently for him to finish unveiling his cathartic, Dr. Phil wisdom, but I soon realize he's got nothing more to add. "You're kidding, right? *Just do it?* We don't live in a Nike commercial, Colin. I can't just slam-dunk a ball and *poof* everything's all better."

"Whoa. You're way overthinking this. Obviously there's no magic formula that's going to make it all disappear. You said some pretty stupid shit and he's really pissed. It's definitely going to take some time. But you can own up to it and make sure it never happens again. 'Just doing it' simply means you commit to being the person you want to be and . . . doing it."

"But what's the point if he can't even stand to be around me long enough to realize that I have 'just done it'?"

He tips his head slightly as if carefully considering my question. After a long pause he says, "Who exactly are you just doing it for?"

He must recognize the WTF in my expression, because he quickly clarifies his question.

"Do you want to make it right for Quinn or for yourself? Because if this is just about looking good for Quinn, don't waste your time."

His question hits me as gently as a boulder to the head. Obviously Quinn is the motivation for change, but when I think back to those hideous things he said about me, I can't help but wonder if any of them are true. Or does it just feel that way because someone I actually care about said them?

"So what's it gonna be, Cricket? Are you gonna just do it?"

FIFTEEN

By the time we conclude our mountaintop therapy session, Colin's got me so convinced that I can transform myself into the person I want to be, I could probably run for congress. Or prom court.

We arrive back at the mess hall just in time for the evening hike, and all my hopefulness disappears the moment I spot Quinn. As feared, his eyes sweep across me like I'm a vapor in the wind.

"What crawled up his ass?" Fantine asks, observing Quinn's mood.

"I'll fill you in later," I say. "It's pretty ugly."

"All right, gang! Who's ready to hike?" Rainbow calls the campers to attention, reminding them to stay on the trail and use their whistles if they get separated, before releasing them on their weekly, semi-unsupervised nighttime stroll. I step back to make room for her as she passes by, but the distance doesn't prevent her from making another one of her unappreciated comments. "Go easy on the bug spray, Cricket. DEET is not your friend."

Annoyed by her instruction, I just roll my eyes.

Colin finishes loading the backpacks with enough snacks, batteries, and first-aid equipment to sustain a militia group for a few months, while Fantine makes one last trip to the bathroom. With no task of my own to complete, I just stand here and pretend that Quinn being halfway down the path, sandwiched between Claire and cock 'n' balls Chase, isn't bothering me.

"You ready, Cricket?" Colin says.

"Ready as I'll ever be."

"Cool. Here's your pack." He takes the red JanSport from Fantine, who already has an identical yellow one strapped to her back. "And here's your flashlight. Do you need a whistle, or do you think you can survive without one?"

"I think I can manage," I say, slinging the pack over my shoulders as I fall into line between the two of them.

"What the hell happened with you and Quinn?" Fantine asks, no more than a yard into our hike. "I've never seen him so pissed off before."

I send Colin a pleading look, but only receive an encouraging nod in return.

"Okay," I mutter. "You asked for it."

I start out slowly, unveiling the gentler, less deplorable facts first. Like the reason why I fainted the first day, and the truth about my botched escape plan Saturday night. Fantine doesn't seem fazed, so I continue on with the stuff about Quinn and his brother, and the awful things I said that I wish I could take back.

"Pumpkin heads," she says.

"What?" Colin and I say in unison.

"Pumpkin heads," she says again, shaking her head. "That's what I used to call them. Can you believe that?" She turns and looks at me with disbelief in her eyes. "I took this job thinking I was going to be helping blind kids. Don't ask me why, but when they said disabled teens I just assumed they'd be blind. When I got here I almost crapped myself. I'd never been around kids with disabilities like these and I definitely wasn't prepared for it."

"I hear that," I say under my breath.

"I still remember that first night," she continues. "I called my cousin and told her some of the kids here looked like they were wearing pumpkins on their heads. Man, it makes me sick just thinking about it now. Anyway, it wasn't until a few days later when Meredith broke her arm and wanted me to ride in the ambulance with her that everything changed. I've never been so scared or protective of someone in my life."

Protective. Just like Quinn.

"We all have our moments," Colin adds, air quoting the word *moments*. "Remember Scotty Marshall?"

"Oh my God!" Fantine shrieks, forgetting her grievances. "How could I forget? That was the funniest thing I've ever seen."

"Wait, I'm supposed to ask you about him," I say. "Who was he?"

"Scotty Marshall was *my* moment," he says with a roll of his dark eyes. "He was a drop-in camper I had my second year—"

"Wait, what's a drop-in camper?" I interrupt, wondering if

there's yet another disability I'm clueless about.

"It's someone like Aidan," Fantine says. "They're physically impaired but have no mental disabilities. Rainbow offers it up to college students who are thinking about going into special education. It's just a different way to get familiar with disabled kids outside the classroom."

I quickly flip through my mental Rolodex, and determine that Aidan is one of Colin's campers—the surprisingly cute guy who maneuvers his wheelchair better than Tony Hawk does a skateboard.

"Anyway," Colin continues, "we got along great, and for the most part he was a really cool kid. The only weird thing about him was that he didn't wear shorts—just jeans or sweats."

"All the time?" I ask.

"All the time," Fantine mumbles under her breath. I glance over at her and see that she's working really hard not to laugh.

I turn back to Colin. "Even when he slept?"

"Yep," he says.

"Why would he do that? It's so hot out here."

Colin opens his mouth to respond, but he's too slow. "Because he had a prosthetic leg!" Fantine says, unable to contain herself any longer. She bursts into a fit of laughter while my eyes grow wide.

"He what?"

"He did," Colin says. "He had a prosthetic leg and apparently everybody knew about it but me—because I woke up next to it one morning and practically shit myself. I thought somebody had been murdered. It was lying right next to me on the pillow with ketchup splattered all over it to make it look like blood—"

"Colin came running out of the cabin bare-assed screaming, *Call 9-1-1! There's a leg in my bed! There's a leg in my bed!* I swear to God that was the funniest thing I've ever seen," Fantine says, swiping tears from her cheeks. Her amusement is contagious because now I'm laughing, too.

"Yeah, well, it was embarrassing. But it was definitely an eye-opener."

"How so?" I say. "Realizing that you shouldn't sleep naked?"

"Well, yeah, there's that. But it wasn't until I learned that my own campers were the ones who convinced Scotty to pull the prank, that I realized I'd been operating under a whole 'us' and 'them' mentality. Just knowing that disabled kids were down for pulling something like that evened everything out. We were all on the same playing field."

"Well, there's more to it for me," I say, my amusement disappearing. "There has to be. I already had my moment and I blew it because I was too freaked out to recognize what was happening."

"What moment are you talking about?" Colin says.

"*The Karate Kid.* Cricket loves Daniel-san, Cricket loves Daniel-san. Remember?"

"Oh please," Fantine says. "*Karate Kid* wasn't your moment—it was damn funny but it wasn't your moment. What you need to remember is we all figure it out in our own way, on our own time. And *you've* got seventeen years of prima donna shoved up your ass, so it's probably gonna take a little bit longer to shake it loose."

"This, by far, is the most painfully enlightening day in the history of the world."

"Just take it one step at a time," says Colin. "Before you know it, you'll love these kids more than a Versace red tag sale."

"Right," I say unconvincingly. "As if Versace's ever on sale."

SIXTEEN

"Eating breakfast isn't supposed to be a painful experience."

"Try and relax," Fantine says in a tone more motherly than I'd think her capable of. "It's just like Colin said, one step at a time. All you have to do is get through breakfast. Then it's just us girls the rest of the day. Besides, maybe one night of treating you like the plague was all he needed to get it out of his system."

I walk into the dining hall and see that Quinn has selected a seat at the corner table with his back toward the rest of the room. By the way he's inhaling his Frosted Flakes, he won't be there long. "I'm thinking one night won't cut it."

"It'll be okay," she says. "He'll come around, and if he doesn't, screw him."

If only I shared her flippant attitude.

Fantine makes her way to her usual spot at the table closest to the door, while I let Meredith roll into her slot and Claire pour herself into her chair. Once they're settled, I squeeze into the seat between them. The fact that this feels normal now is disturbing.

"Have yoooooou decided what weeeeee're doooing for the shooow?"

Up until a few days ago, sticking around for battle of the bands wasn't even an option. To suggest that I'd even thought of what to perform . . . "Uh, no. Did you have an idea?" I regret asking the question the second it leaves my mouth.

"Yes!" Claire interrupts, squeezing my arm. "We have a good idea."

"But we neeeeeed to talk in priiiiiivate," Meredith adds, before attacking my other arm.

"Okay, okay, just chill," I say, shaking them loose. "We'll talk about it this afternoon."

I'm reminded that this afternoon marks the first time I will officially be on my own with Claire and Meredith. It feels more like underpaid babysitting than the death sentence I would have expected.

"You will love this idea," Claire says. "It's my best ever. And I have a lot of them." She's nodding her head so fast I'm surprised it doesn't pop off.

"Fine. Great. Whatever. Can I eat now?" I pour some 2% into my bowl and am spooning up my first magically delicious clover, when Quinn's voice draws my attention across the room.

"I'll meet you guys out there," he says to the boys at his table. "And be sure to tell Colin you need to collect some rocks on the way. You'll need at least five for the experiment."

"You got it, boss!" one of the boys answers eagerly, while the others nod their oversize heads in agreement.

"Cool. See you in a few." Quinn slides his chair under the table, offering me a glimpse of those broad shoulders I love so much. He pauses, like he's thinking he might sneak a peek at me over his shoulder.

I sit up a little straighter, quickly adjusting my hair so it falls over my shoulder like Rapunzel's. The anticipation of those beautiful blue eyes landing on me is almost too much to stand. He's just about to turn his head . . . and then he strides out of the room without so much as a glance in my direction.

My shoulders sag as that same, deep-seated ache returns to my throat. Colin was right. This is going to be hard.

* * *

After a sad and visually repulsive attempt at water aerobics, we start down yet another wheelchair-friendly path toward the craft hut where the girls will continue to work on their watercolor paintings. Fantine's leading the way, her campers providing her the appropriate amount of personal space, while my two BFFs are still glued to my sides—right where they've been all freaking morning.

"Whaaaaaaat's wroooong, Cricket?" Meredith asks. She wraps her tiny hand around mine before I have a chance to object.

"Nothing," I say, glaring down at her. "Isn't it hard to steer that thing with one hand?"

"Noooooo. I caaan do it with one fiiiinger now. Want to seeeee?"

"No," I answer quickly. "I believe you."

"What's wrong? We can help you." Claire takes my other hand in hers. I've just developed claustrophobia.

"Nothing's wrong." I try to wiggle my hands away from theirs, but they've got some handicapped ninja death grip on me. "Sometimes people just have a bad day, that's all."

"Does this haaaaaave to dooooo with Quinn?"

"No."

"Are you suuuuure?"

"Yes, Meredith. Stop being nosy."

"I'm juuuust trying tooooo help. My mom saaays I'm suuuuper good at helping people. I waaaaatch Oprah reeeeruns every day. Youuuuuuu can learn a lot from Oprah."

Count to ten, Cricket. . . .

"Good for you, Meredith," I say, releasing an exhausted breath. "But like I said, I'm *fine*."

My hands are growing sweatier and my patience thinner with every step. Being sandwiched between these two on a perfectly good Thursday was definitely not on my playlist for this summer.

"Oh . . ." Claire pipes up several minutes later. "You have your period, right?"

"What?"

"It's okay. Girls are bitches on their period. My big sister said she'd kill me once."

Claire getting a death threat. There's a shocker.

"I don't have my period, Claire," I say through gritted teeth. "And what kind of question is that anyway? It's none of your business. Or yours"—I glare down at Meredith—"I'm having a bad day. That's it. Just a *really* bad day. Now please stop talking about it."

They both go absolutely silent, and for the first time in twenty minutes I can actually hear myself think. Apparently letting them know who's the boss is all they needed.

"I know!" Claire says out of nowhere. "You need Midol! I have some in my bag."

"I loooooove Midol."

"Oh my God!" I shriek, shaking my hands free of theirs. "What is wrong with you guys? I don't need any freaking Midol! *I don't have my period!*" I stomp away from them, arms flailing like I walked through a spiderweb. Those two are insane if they think I'm going to let them try to mother-hen me.

Thankfully the activities in the craft shed are distracting enough that at least thirty minutes pass before either of them speaks again.

"Ta-da!" Claire says, stepping away from her painting easel.

"My, my," Fantine says, her brow arched above a scrutinizing eye. "It's always the quiet, unassuming ones, isn't it?"

Curious, I walk over to survey the masterpiece under review. How Fantine is able to keep a straight face is beyond me. I'm about ready to pee myself when I see the anatomically exaggerated, pastel rendering of the world's biggest penis.

"Claire," I say, trying my best not to snort. "It's . . . it's . . ."

"Huge?" she says encouragingly.

"Yes!" I erupt. "It's *huge*. Why did you paint that?"

"I wanted to make you happy," she says, her round cheeks blushing. "A giant wiener makes everyone happy!"

The laughter in the tiny shed is contagious. Fantine is hinged over at the waist cackling, and Meredith is shaking so hard I fear she may topple out of her wheelchair. Normally, I'd be dabbing at the streaks of mascara staining my face, but today I don't care. The whole scene is a hysterical nightmare. Before I can stop myself, I throw my arm around Claire's wide shoulder and give her a hug.

"Thanks, Claire. I really needed that."

"You're welcome," she says, still beaming. "But I do have Midol."

"Okay," I say. "I'll keep that in mind."

SEVENTEEN

I t takes a solid twenty minutes for the giant purple penis experience to run its course, and now we're facing the arduous task of cleaning up our mess.

Since Fantine is busy showing the girls how to drape their paintings so the bugs don't attack them, I decide to rinse the brushes and palettes. Arms loaded, I head outside and shuffle toward the sinks at the backside of the building, carefully balancing the load I should have taken in two trips.

"Heads up!"

The scream coming from behind more than startles me, and I quickly look over my shoulder just in time to catch a blurry glimpse of Aidan and his wheelchair of death flying down a hill heading straight for me.

The impact is abrupt and knocks me off my feet and sailing into the tower of palettes. Aidan skids into the craft shed, denting its rusted exterior, though miraculously staying upright in his chair.

"Holy crap, Cricket, are you okay?" Aidan asks, laughing like he just climbed off a white-knuckler at Six Flags.

"What the hell is wrong with you? Couldn't you see me

standing there?"

"I'm sorry," he says, still amused. "I was trying to beat my time down the hill and I lost control on some loose gravel. I tried to warn you, but I guess you didn't hear me."

"Obviously!"

"Are you okay?" Quinn suddenly appears from behind me. He's completely out of breath and glistening with sweat. "Didn't you hear us yelling at you?"

"Yeah, I heard you," I say. I'm too pissed to enjoy the fact that he's speaking to me. "About half a second before Speedy Gonzales over here ran into me. I didn't even have time to move!"

"I'm really sorry," Aidan says again. "If it makes you feel any better, I think the shed took a harder hit than you did."

I deliver him another scathing look before surveying my own injuries. No fresh blood and all of my limbs are intact, though they're covered in about a thousand different colors of paint.

"What's going on?" Fantine pushes her way through the growing crowd. I could smack her for the look she's wearing. "Damn, girl. You look like gay pride parade threw up on you."

"Thank you!" I say, shooting her my best death glare. This time she actually flinches. What's worse is that Quinn is just staring at me, and now he's got this annoying little grin on his face.

"I really am sorry, Cricket," Aidan says, straight-faced and focused on me. "By the time I came over the hill and realigned myself in the chair, I was practically on top of you. If I'd have turned harder left to avoid you, I would've wiped out for sure."

Every fiber in my body begs to throw a tantrum, but it dawns on me that this could actually be a *just do it* moment—and Quinn's here to witness it!

I take a deep breath before hoisting my colorful body off the ground. "It's okay," I say, pushing a clump of purple hair from my eyes so I can see him. "I know it was an accident, Aidan. I'm sorry I yelled at you. Are you okay?"

"Oh, I'm all good. I've been looking for an excuse to get close to you for the last week. I guess I know what it takes, huh?" He leans back in his seat so the two big wheels support the entire weight of his chair, and spins around in a perfect circle on the colorful dirt.

The crowd bursts into applause, earning Aidan several high fives from his new fans. Everyone's having a great time now—everyone except Quinn. He just fired a lethal glare right at me before storming off in a huff.

✳ ✳ ✳

After an hour with my loofah, I finally emerge from the shower as my regular Caucasian self, not a drop of paint left anywhere on my body. Rather than take the time to blow-dry my hair, I tie it back in a pony and slip on my Ed Hardy rhinestone cap.

I stroll out of the bathroom and back into the world of blue curbed parking, and find Aidan waiting for me with a fistful of wildflowers in his hand and a hopeful look on his face.

"A peace offering," he says, handing me the sad-looking bouquet.

"Oh, that's sweet, Aidan. You didn't need to do that." I take the flowers with a strange combination of trepidation and pleasure while scanning the perimeter to see if we still have an audience.

"They're all at lunch," he says. "I wanted to hang back and make sure you were okay."

"Oh right. Yeah, I'm good. The whole getting knocked on my ass thing threw me a little. But seriously, I'm fine now."

"You sure about that?" he asks, his dark eyes narrowing into thin lines beneath the afternoon sun. "'Cause it seemed to me like the second Quinn took off, so did your good mood."

"What are you talking about? Why would I care that Quinn took off?"

"Come on, Cricket," he says as he folds his tan arms across his chest. "There's obviously something going on with you two. Quinn's a cool guy and everything, but I'm more than willing to kick his ass for you."

I laugh. "All right." I sit down on the nearest tree trunk bench. I'm not sure if it's the wilting flowers in my hand, or if it's because his overly confident attitude reminds me of all the guys I know back home, but there's something about Aidan that makes me want to trust him. "I'll fill you in, but it has to stay between us, okay?"

"Of course," he assures me, rolling closer. "Just between us."

"You have to let me get it all out first, okay? Because you're going to want to yell at me, or hit me or something, but just let me finish."

"Sure," he says. "But I'm not going to hit you."

"Don't bet on it."

It's sort of sad how long it takes, but when I've finally unloaded all my emotional baggage, Aidan says, "Wow. You're the biggest bitch I've ever met."

His words are harsh and pierce at my insides, but the grin slowly inching across his face leads me to believe he might not actually mean them. "We should have you arrested, or I don't know, tarred and feathered in the center of town—"

"Ugh, don't be a jerk," I say. "You asked me to tell you and I did. You could at least take it seriously."

"I'm sorry," he says. "I promise I'm taking you seriously. I just think you're being way too hard on yourself, that's all."

"You do?"

"Well, it's not like you're the first person to make fun of handicapped people." He recognizes that his response catches me off guard. "What?" he says. "It's true. And until two years ago, I probably wasn't much different from you," he says in a slightly softer tone. "I had a normal life; I had just turned seventeen, was playing varsity baseball, hanging with the all the right people, until one night I made a really bad decision and screwed it all up."

"What happened?"

"A buddy and I were at a party and we were too drunk to drive home. A couple of seniors said they'd take us, so we hopped in the car with them. Unfortunately we were too faded to realize they were as drunk as we were. One minute we're rocking out to an old Metallica song, cruising through the Taco Bell drive-thru, and the next there's the loudest noise I've ever heard and the whole world goes black. I woke up in the hospital a week later. My spinal cord had been severed in two places."

"Oh my God. You could have been killed."

He nods.

"What happened to the other guys?"

"My best friend ended up with a punctured lung and a few broken bones, but the other guys walked away perfectly fine. I got the worst of it."

"I hope somebody took care of that driver in a dark alley. What a dick! He should have known he was too drunk to drive. You need to sue him or something." I pause to take a breath. "What's so funny?"

"You," he says. "And it's not that you're funny, you're just . . . cute. I mean—the way you're responding is cute," he says, quickly trying to cover his slip-up. "Look," he says. "I appreciate you wanting to defend me, but it doesn't bother me so much now."

"Then why did you tell me?"

"Because I wanted you to know that being uncomfortable around disabled people doesn't make you a horrible person—it makes you honest. It makes you real."

Once again, his simplistic response catches me by surprise.

"What you said sucks, but I bet most people think the same things you did. They just don't admit it because they're too scared. That's what happens when you live in a vacuum and aren't exposed to different kinds of people. You react out of fear, or self-protection or something."

A sour taste begins welling up in my mouth, as Quinn's bubble-living comments collide with Aidan's obvious wisdom.

"I'm speaking from experience, here," he continues. "I wasn't lying when I said I was just like you—I was a total dick to people, too. Handicapped people," he clarifies. "I said really shitty things, made stupid gestures, and then just like that"—he snaps his fingers—"I was one of them. I was the one other people stared at. I was the one whose friends bailed when they realized I couldn't do everything the same way anymore. Everything's different when the shoe's on the other foot."

"So you're saying I need to play in traffic so I can end up in a wheelchair? That'll help me get over myself?"

"No, smart ass," he says. "I'm saying you should be grateful that a summer camp pretty boy helped you figure it out. Bruised egos and broken hearts definitely suck, but I assure you getting hit by an F-150 at forty-five miles an hour is a much harder way to figure it out."

If I didn't already feel like queen of the bitches, I certainly do now. He's sitting here without the use of his legs, and *I'm* the one who's whining like a pathetic baby.

"Okay," I say. "So somehow you've managed to be okay with this crappy hand life has dealt you, but that doesn't explain why you're here. All the other kids seem to have some mental . . ."

"Impairments?"

"Sure. So clearly you're not *impaired*. How did you end up here?"

"My mom and Rainbow did some student teaching together back in the day. She knew about the camp, and when I mentioned I was thinking about majoring in special education, she gave her a call and, voilà. Here I am."

"Apparently Rainbow knows everybody's parents," I mumble.

"She knows your folks too?"

"My dad," I say. "Not to mention a shitload of other personal stuff."

He cocks his head slightly, confused.

"It's nothing," I say, shaking off my personal irritations. "So you're a . . . drop-in camper?"

"Right," he says, completely unaware of how hard I had to search my memory bank to come up with that. "But I don't really think of it as camping. I'm approaching this like I'm an in-the-trenches observer, if that makes any sense."

"Like an experiment?"

"Eh, more like personal development. I don't think I'll be a very good teacher if I have any hang-ups about the kids I'm teaching. Sharing my life with them puts us all on the same playing field."

"You make it sound so easy."

He reels his head back. "Do you think I like building birdhouses out of Popsicle sticks? I have to check my pride at the door every morning. *Every* morning. But that's kind of the whole point, right? Getting over yourself . . ."

I shake my head. "How can you only be a year older than me and like a thousand times smarter?"

"Trust me, I'm not that smart. I've just had a couple years to adjust to this. You've only had a week." I feel his hand cover mine; it's calloused but comforting "So what do you think? Are you gonna stick it out the rest of the summer?"

It's crazy how obvious an answer can be when the question is asked by someone other than yourself.

"Yeah," I say. "I'm going to stick around."

"Cool," he says. "Everybody deserves a second chance to make things right, Cricket. Even you. And if Quinn doesn't realize that, then he's the jerk."

"You sound like Fantine."

"Fantine's a badass."

"Yeah." I chuckle. "She is."

Neither of us says anything for a while. We just sit with his hand covering mine, soaking up the warm day. It's the first time since the blowup with Quinn that I feel the slightest bit good about myself. It's also the first time since I've been here that I'm not uncomfortable that the person sitting next to me can't walk.

"Cricket," he says. "If Quinn turns out to be a total dick about this—do I even stand a chance?"

I feel my cheeks flush behind my growing smile. "You'll kick his ass first, right?"

EIGHTEEN

"Oh my God, this shit *is* bananas!" Staring at the tiny screen of my iPhone, Fantine erupts into a fit of laughter while I try to suffocate myself with my pillow. "How did you let them talk you into this?"

"It was Meredith. She wore me down."

"*You* caved for Meredith?"

"She so played the handicapped card. Can you believe that? She's all, *yooooou wouldn't say noooo to a kid in a wheelchair, woooooooould you?* What else could I do?"

"Well, you could have suggested a different song. Not that I don't love some Gwen Stefani, but 'Hollaback' is kind of old. Plus it's tough with all that spelling. Do you really think Claire can spell bananas that fast?"

"Of course she can't," I say. "I tried to convince her but she was dead set on it. Besides, I'm trying to be the new and improved Cricket, remember? I figured I shouldn't push it. I mean, she can't help her condition, right?"

She pauses the video with a tap of her finger and looks over at me. "What condition?"

"Whatever it is that makes her think we're still living in 2008."

Fantine's eyes grow wide and her mouth falls open just a smidge. "You're kidding, right?"

"About what?"

"Oh my God!" she says, collapsing against her pillow, laughing. "She doesn't have a *condition*, Cricket. The girl's just nuts."

"Wait . . . what?" I sit up on my bed so I can face her. "She doesn't have some kind of neurological disorder? I mean, beyond the cerebral palsy?"

She shakes her head.

"So the whole Hannah Montana fixation is just . . . she's just . . ."

"Like I said, she's nuts." Fantine snorts. "Something really good must have happened to her five years ago because she doesn't want to get herself out of the time warp. But I assure you, there's no condition causing that. It's a straight-up WTF situation when it comes to Meredith and what she likes."

Feeling every part the idiot, I bury my face in my hands. So much for being enlightened.

"Ooh! This move right here is amazing. Check this out, you *have* to do this one." I stomp across the short distance to Fantine's bed and collapse down beside her. "See how Gwen does this snake thing against the dashboard?" she says, pointing to the "Hollaback Girl" video she's watched at least a dozen times already. "You totally need to do that. Quinn will go crazy just watching you."

"I doubt it," I say, nudging her closer to the wall so we can share her pillow. "Did you see him at the pool tonight? He won't even look at me." I take out my ponytail, give my head a scratch, and settle further into the pillow. Gwen's voice is starting to give me a headache. "This morning at the craft shed it almost seemed like he was getting over it, but then all of a sudden he just froze up. Like he remembered he hated me."

"He doesn't hate you," she says, pausing the music again. "He just doesn't know how to go about forgiving you. Some guys are stupid like that. And from what Colin's told me, Quinn has a particularly hard time letting things go. Besides, I saw you having a pretty good time with Aidan anyway."

"Please, Aidan's my . . . friend."

"Friend. Right."

"He is!" I smack her arm. "We're just friends. Or becoming friends. Besides, he knows how I feel about Quinn."

"I'm just saying I think he'd be more than happy to take you for a ride on his wheelchair."

"You're disgusting," I say. She just laughs. "I can't think about Quinn right now anyway. I've got other things to worry about."

"Like what?"

"Like how the hell we are going to pull off a three-girl reenactment of *that*." I point to the frozen image of Gwen on the screen, her washboard abs and bright red lips gleaming under the Hollywood sun. I might as well kill myself now. "The majority of that video is dancing."

"Yeah, so?"

"Do you live under a rock? Have you completely forgotten who I've got to work with?"

"Why, Constance, whatever are you talking about?" Her grin borders on that fine line between a smile and all-out hysterics.

"You know exactly what I'm talking about," I say in a low voice, aware that the subjects in question are asleep in the next room. "Claire can hardly stand up without knocking someone over, and Meredith . . . I mean, seriously. She's in a wheelchair! I don't know about you, but I've never seen someone in a wheelchair dance. I'm telling you, Fantine, the whole thing is going to be a freakin' disaster, and yours truly will be center stage looking like the queen of the freak show. Tell me again why counselors have to participate?"

"That's just how it is. Each counselor performs with their group and then one lucky leader, that'd be you, gets to supervise all the campers in one big group performance. Think of how much fun that's gonna be!"

"This totally sucks," I say, kicking my heels into the bed. I'm about five seconds away from completely losing it, when I hear a small voice outside the curtain.

"Cricket?"

"Uh . . . yeah?" Fantine and I exchange a glance, scrambling to sit up in the bed. "Who is it?"

Claire's very round, sunburned face appears from a gap in the curtain. "It's me," she says warily. "Can I come in?"

"Sure," I say, motioning her inside. "What's going on?"

She thunders through the doorway, her *Twilight* nightgown trailing behind her. Her hair is matted and her eyes are red.

"Are you okay?"

"I had a bad dream. It scared me."

Comforting people isn't really my gig, but I remember back to how Carolyn handled these situations when I was little.

"Do you want to talk about it?" I say, patting the foot of the bed. "Sometimes talking about it makes it not so scary."

"Okay," she says, and drops down right beside me, forcing me to shift to my right so I'm not crushed.

"What happened?"

"I was at the archery range with James and Shia LaBeouf—"

"Shia LaBeouf?" I'm not sure how but I manage to stifle my laughter.

She nods. "I like him. He's cute."

"He totally is," I say.

"He's super cute." Fantine nods in agreement.

"Everybody was shooting, but the targets weren't right. They were purple Jell-O, and wherever the arrow landed is how much Jell-O you had to eat." I cover my mouth trying not to laugh. This sounds more like a Tim Burton movie than a nightmare. "And then Rainbow showed up and she was covered with roly polies. They were crawling all over her, and she was screaming at all of us. She said we had to eat all the Jell-O or she'd throw us in the roly poly pit. I hate roly polies, Cricket!"

Without hesitation, I put an arm around her shoulder. "It was just a dream," I say. "Dreams are crazy and stupid sometimes, but they can't hurt you."

"And neither can roly polies," Fantine adds.

"Yeah," I say. "Roly polies are just cute little bugs who curl up into balls when they're scared. They definitely can't hurt you." Fantine and I exchange another glance, while Claire proceeds to snot all over my shirt.

"Do you think you can go back to bed?" I ask when she's finally stopped snorting.

She nods. "Yeah, I can go to bed. Thanks, Cricket."

"No problem," I say. "Good night, Claire."

We wait for her to disappear into the main room before I climb back into my own bed.

"That was one jacked-up dream," Fantine says. "Don't you ever wonder why we dream what we do?"

"In this instance, no."

"So you think Jell-O target practice is normal?"

"No, it's definitely weird," I say, adjusting the scratchy covers. "I'm talking about the part of the dream that really scared her. The Rainbow part."

"Why?" She props herself up on one elbow and narrows her

eyes on me. "You said it didn't bother you that your dad had a financial interest in the camp, but you're always grumbling about Rainbow under your breath. So which is it? Do you care or don't you?"

"No"—I blow out a sigh—"I don't care what he does with his money."

"So what's your problem then?"

"My problem is her. Half the time she treats me like a bratty kid, because, if you remember, she told me I was one. And then she's commenting on my personal life. She knows stuff about me, Fantine. Stuff I've never told her—or anyone here."

"Like?"

"Like . . . meat."

"Meat? I thought we weren't talking about Quinn anymore."

"Ugh, you are so gross. I'm talking about meat like from a cow. Tonight at dinner she said she knew I wasn't a big red meat eater but wanted me to try Sam's beef anyway because it was really good."

"It *was* good."

"Yeah, it was. But you're missing the point. I never told her that I don't eat a lot of red meat. She just knew it. How could she possibly know that about me?"

"A lot of people don't eat red meat, Cricket." She dims the lantern on our bookshelf before collapsing into her pillow with a sigh. "She probably just figured you for one of those trendy vegetarian, experimental lesbian types. I wouldn't read into it."

"You're wrong," I say firmly. "She knows things about me and my life, things she shouldn't know. And it's not just the meat thing. There have been a lot of other little things. This morning after breakfast she told me Sam was making cream puffs for dessert tomorrow because she knows they're my favorite. And yesterday I heard her tell Pete that I used to sleepwalk—"

"Whoa, take a breath. So she knows a lot about you, so what? You either ask her how she knows you so well, or you ignore her. I don't care which you do, but you gotta pick one because you're starting to ramble again. I'm about ready to rip my ears off."

"Well, thanks for the help. And here I thought *I* was the camp bitch."

"What can I say."

"Fine. I won't complain to you anymore. But if something goes down with her you better have my back."

"Oh, I got your back. I'll make sure the Mystery Machine is gassed up and ready for action whenever you need me."

"Sometimes I really hate you," I say, my grin going unappreciated by the dark room.

"I know. I hate you, too."

"And I am *so* not a lesbian."

NINETEEN

Up until my arrival at camp, I'd been waking up on the same time frame as the cable guy: somewhere between ten and two. This six-thirty crap should be reserved for high school dropouts with paper routes.

I lumber out of bed, noting that Fantine's wool blanket is already spread smooth and tight across her empty bed, and grab my bathroom supplies off the tiny wooden shelf. I make my way through the bunkhouse, saying halfhearted good mornings to the campers, and walk out the door into the already warm morning.

"H-h-he-hello, Cricket," James says, crutching by me with a fish-shaped oven mitt on his hand. "How are you t-t-today?"

"Peachy-keen, James. How are you?"

He stops suddenly and scratches his head with his salmon-covered hand. "Happy and t-t-tall," he finally says. "I am h-h-h-happy and t-t-tall today."

"That's good, James. Happy and tall beats the hell out of tired and bloated."

I walk through the restroom's wide doorway, making my way

past the low sinks and the toilets with supporting hand rails to the middle changing stall, where I strip down to my birthday suit. It's a sad, sad sight. My once smooth skin is covered in bruises, Band-Aids, and dime-sized mosquito bites. But miracles happen when scalding hot water and scented shower gel come together. Within a minute I feel awake, alert, and slightly less disgusted with the day that lies ahead.

Fantine and the girls are waiting for me at the foot of the bunkhouse steps when I emerge from the bathroom.

"Hurry up!" Claire says. "We can't be late for breakfast."

"I'll catch up with you guys in a minute," I say, directing my comment to Fantine. "I need to put some new Band-Aids on the blisters."

"Sounds good. Let's go, ladies. We'll save Cricket a spot."

While they go on their way to the mess hall, I run up the steps and into the bunkhouse. I plop on my bed, brushing off my already dusty feet, and trade out my Bieber Band-Aids for some equally cool Pooh Bear ones. I tug on some socks, carefully slide my feet into my shoes, and am nearly to the door when I hear someone on the rickety front porch.

I push the door open and peek my head around the corner. "Oh boy," I mumble, suddenly feeling sick. "Hi," I say in a voice that's about four degrees south of nervous.

"Hey," Quinn says back. "We need to talk."

"Okay?" I step out onto the porch and tug the door shut

behind me. "What do we need to talk about?"

"You and Aidan."

"Me and . . . Aidan?"

"Yeah," he crosses his arms. "I just want you to know that I think it's really crappy you're using him just to get to me. It's not going to make me jealous if that's what you were hoping for."

Well now, if this isn't an Edward/Bella/Jacob moment, I don't know what is. Where is Claire when I need her?

"Aidan is my *friend*," I say, struggling not to crack a smile. "I'm not using him for anything, and I'm certainly not trying to make you jealous."

"Oh really?" He drops his sly guy demeanor by taking off his sunglasses. "You expect me to believe that all of a sudden you're going to be best friends with somebody in a wheelchair? How stupid do you think I am?"

"Well, at this point I don't think you're stupid, but I am starting to think you're an asshole. Contrary to what you might think, my existence here doesn't completely revolve around you."

"Oh, that's rich, Cricket. You have a come-to-Jesus moment two days ago and now you're suddenly a changed person? I'm the asshole?"

"Are you comparing yourself to Jesus now? First Efron and now Jesus . . ."

"Of course not. I'm saying that if you expect me to believe you've done a complete one-eighty just because of something

I said, then you must think I'm an idiot. People don't change overnight."

"For the record," I say, fighting a strong urge to poke my finger in his chest. "It wasn't something you *said* to me, it was something you *screamed* at me—in my face. And I never said I was changed, but I am working on it. A fact that seems to be acceptable to everybody else in this dump except for you."

His eyes soften just slightly and for a moment I catch a glimpse of the guy I haven't seen in a while. "Why do you care what I think of you anyway? According to Rainbow, you're leaving as soon as your dad gets back."

"Ah, yes. Good ole Rainbow!" I say with sarcasm. "Actually, I've decided to stay. Not that it makes any difference to you now, but . . . yeah, I'm going to stick around and see this thing through." I feel that stupid knot of emotion building up again, but rather than burst into tears, I push by him. "You know what the really sad part is?" I call over my shoulder. "I'm doing exactly what you told me to do. I'm trying to be the person *I* want to be, and you can't even acknowledge that."

TWENTY

Over the course of the next twenty-four hours, Claire, Meredith, and I spend more time analyzing Gwen Stefani and every freaking second of the "Hollaback Girl" video than even her most faithful stalker.

To my surprise, both of them have memorized the lyrics, though Claire still trips up every time we have to spell out the word *bananas*. Our choreography, on the other hand, is worse than I feared it would be. Claire maneuvering her enormous body in a cheerleader's uniform is nauseating. And as for Meredith, well, it seems her athletic skills are limited to the pool. The girl's got zero rhythm. I can't even imagine how much worse she'd be if her legs actually worked.

Fantine and her girls have decided to perform "Call Me Maybe," while Colin's group is doing "Radioactive." If I didn't know better, I'd think Ryan Seacrest was paying the bills around here instead of my dad.

And as far as Quinn's group, well, I suppose that will remain a mystery until the big night. Since our little chat on the porch the other morning, I've had very little interaction with him. He has muttered a few words in my general direction, though I hardly consider "damn, it's hot today" to be very personal. All in all, I'd have to say Quinn is convinced I'm a self-centered, high-maintenance bitch who's never going to change. Which sucks, because I think I'm making pretty good progress, myself. I didn't even laugh when Claire started barking this morning. Swear to God.

But, as much as I'd like to dream the day away, imagining that Quinn and I have forgiven each other and we're back to our late night, PG-13 activities, I actually do have other things to think about. The group performance being the most obvious, and Rainbow's knowledge of my personal life, the most infuriating.

Since I'm hoping my father, who should arrive home today, will be able to cast some light on the Rainbow situation, I decide to try to remedy the first dilemma I'm faced with.

At Fantine's suggestion, I stop by the kitchen to see if Sam has any ideas about a final performance. At first I've got no idea why my bunkmate would make such a ridiculous recommendation, but seeing Sam's eyes light up when my question hits his ears, I remember what Quinn told me about him. First, that he was a brilliant chef. Second, that he knew more about Madonna than Madonna herself.

"Do 'Vogue,'" he says. "It's weird, and people like it."

"'Vogue'? Like from the '80s?"

"March 20. March 20, 1990," he says, not picking up on an ounce of my sarcasm. "Watch the Blond Ambition Tour DVD.

Japan is the best."

Oh. My. God.

"Um . . . okay," I say. "I guess I can climb the hill and try and download it to my iPad. . . ."

"Don't do that. Borrow mine. I have the DVD and a player in my trailer."

"Okay, that'd be great," I say. "Maybe I can get it after dinner tonight?"

He nods his head with great consideration. "I like helping you, Cricket. You're a nice lady." His smile is so sincere, I actually find myself reaching toward him to offer him a one-armed hug, but he pulls away before I make contact. For half a second I feel like yet another man is dissing me, but remember Quinn said Sam didn't like to be touched. "That's awesome, Sam," I say, giving him a thumbs-up from a safe distance. "You're helping me out a lot."

"Okay, I have to make dinner now. Good-bye, Cricket."

Before I can give him a parting smile, he pushes through the swinging doors and disappears into the kitchen. I push myself up on my toes and peek at him through the door's tiny round window. I can't help but feel a teeny bit jealous. Sam looks so proud pulling his stained apron over his liver-spotted, gnome head. His life may be simple, but I can tell it's pretty damn good.

* * *

"Stupid Madonna, stupid Madonna," I mutter as I scramble my

way up cell phone hill. I haven't even watched the dumb video yet and "Vogue" is already on instant-replay in my brain.

I crest the hill and begin the task of wandering aimlessly until those beautiful bars appear at the top of the display screen. Within a matter of seconds, I see four little towers pop up and a chime notifies me that I've got a new voice mail and three new text messages. The voice mail is from Carolyn, and all she has to report is that Mr. Katz is now on doggy Prozac. Maybe he'll let me borrow some when I get home. I delete the message after two listens, then move onto the texts. The first is from Katie.

OMG! H2'S DAD HAS PRVT JET! LUV THIS GUY. HAVE FUN W/TARDS. LOL. ALOHA BITCH. XOXO. I find myself sighing and hitting the DELETE button without even responding. Hawaii is making Katie annoying.

The second message is from my dad. HOPE YOU ARE WELL. BUSINESS KEEPS ME IN SPAIN A BIT LONGER. TALK SOON.

The same anticipation that carried me up the hill in under twenty minutes evaporates in less than a breath. My original motivation for speaking with him was to ask about his connection with Rainbow. But it's not until this moment that I realize how badly I wanted to tell him how I was doing here.

I reply to his message with a simple, I'M OK. TALK NXT WEEK, and hit the SEND button. The fact that I even replied to his text will probably send him into cardiac arrest.

I delete my dad's text and scroll to the last message in my inbox. It's from a number I don't recognize . . . a 616 area code. I tap the screen, assuming it's a solicitation to get cheap meds from Canada, and wait for the message to appear.

I SUCK AT APOLOGIES.

My heart starts thumping hard, and that same anxious excitement I haven't felt in days reappears. The phone chimes again, and I look down to find another green message bubble beneath the first.

TURN AROUND.

I whip my head over my shoulder and see Quinn approaching me from just a few yards away.

"Hey," he says in a shaky voice. "Can we talk for a minute?"

My heart is pounding so hard I can't even hear myself think. I just nod.

"I'm sorry I followed you up here. I know this is your private place, but I didn't know how else to get you alone," he says, taking a tentative step closer. "I hope you don't mind."

The way his eyes look in the afternoon sun, he could have killed everyone at camp to get me alone and I'd have been cool with it. "I don't mind."

His expression softens, and he slowly covers some of the distance between us. "I'm not kidding when I say I suck at apologies. I really do. But I owe you one. Actually, I think I probably owe you a couple."

"Go ahead," I say, reminding myself I'm still mad at him. "Apologize."

"Okay . . . I tried to rehearse this, so bear with me." I force myself not to smile. He's cute when he's uncomfortable.

"First off, I know I was a major dick for treating you the way I did the other morning. That wasn't cool, and you didn't deserve it. You can hang out with whoever you want; it's none of my business."

"You're right," I say. "It is none of your business and you were a major dick."

He nods and his gaze shifts away from me to his worn-out Vans.

"I also know that you're trying to change. I mean"—he raises his head to look at me again—"you *are* changing. I can see it and I'm sorry I didn't give you credit for that. I know it hasn't been easy. Cricket, I am *so* sorry," he says again, coming closer. Through blurry eyes I see him reach for me. "I know I don't deserve it, but please, let me try and make this right."

I nod slowly and look into his eyes. "Okay."

"Really?" His relief presents itself in a grateful smile. "That's it? You don't want to chew my ass out first?"

I laugh, while sniffling back my emotions. "A few days ago I would have, but someone gave me some good advice about second chances, so . . ."

Before I can finish my thought, he pulls me against his chest and holds me tightly in his arms. I feel him press his lips against my head.

"I've missed you," I say, breathing in the familiar scent of him.

"I've missed you, too."

We hold each other this way for a while, when Quinn says, "You know, I never finished telling you about my brother the other night. I wanted to, but—"

"Colin told me about Ethan," I cut in, hoping to ease his burden a bit. "And it totally makes sense that you reacted the way you did. The things I said were horrible and the fact that you had all these memories of Ethan, well . . ."

"It's just really hard to talk about."

"Of course," I say, nodding. "He was your brother—you were really close to him."

"Not always." His heavy gaze moves away from me. "I've never actually said this out loud, but I hated him for a long time." He pauses like he's waiting for me to react, but I don't. "My parents waited on him hand and foot," he continues. "I felt like the invisible boy—like I wasn't special enough for them. It was stupid"—he shrugs—"but it was how I felt, even though my parents assured me it wasn't true."

I nod again. "Feeling invisible isn't fun."

"We didn't get close until I was older and able to understand more about his condition."

"And that's when you had to start defending him?"

He nods, returning his attention to me. "He was in the special ed. program at our school, so even though we didn't have any of the same teachers, he was still mainstreamed at certain points in the day. For the most part people were cool. They just sort of ignored the special needs kids, but there were a few guys who loved making their lives hell."

"They made fun of them?"

"On a good day," he says. "The name-calling was the easy part. I'd just tell them to shut up, and they'd usually leave it alone for a while. But before long things started to escalate. They were shoving rotten fruit into his locker, stealing his shoes . . . whatever they could do to get him upset, and in turn, piss me off. It was like they wanted to test me to see how far I'd go to protect him."

A chill races down my spine.

"Ethan begged me to stop defending him—said he was big enough to fight his own battles and didn't need his little brother getting into trouble all the time. It was hard, but I backed off. Things were okay for a while, but then one day it all came to a head. Ethan and his friend were standing in the lunch line and the guys came up and started calling him names again. I knew they were egging me on to see what I'd do, but I kept my cool as best I could. It seemed like they were going to give up, until Chris Davis, the biggest of the three, threw a tray full of food at Ethan. And that's when I snapped. Before I knew what happened, I was knocking over tables and chairs, and found myself in the middle of a brawl, taking on three guys by myself. I was punching, kicking, throwing elbows. . . ."

"Were you hurt?"

"Surprisingly, no," he says, grinning. "I don't know how I came out of that alive. But I guess that's what rage can do to a person." He shakes his head. "We all ended up getting suspended for three days. Looking back, I'm not proud of what I did but I couldn't stop myself. Anyway"—he sighs—"that was the last time I ever fought over him."

"He got pretty pissed at you for getting involved, huh?"

"No. He was actually proud of me for what I did. Said I was braver than Superman," he says, chuckling at the memory. "It was the last time I fought over him because he was admitted into the hospital a few days after that. He was born with a respiratory condition, so every few months he had to go in for treatments." He pauses to catch his breath. "Nobody's really sure how it happened, but he caught an infection while he was there. It's not like it was entirely unexpected—Down's kids are more susceptible to infections then other kids, but we still weren't really prepared for it. I guess you're never really prepared for something like that."

I reach out and take his hand. It's all I can think to do.

"Anyway, that'll be four years ago in December."

"You still miss him a lot, don't you?"

He nods.

"So how are things with your parents now that he's gone?"

"Eh . . . I don't know. We have our moments. I mean, I know they love me and everything, but they're pretty hard on me."

"They're mean to you?"

"No, not mean. It's more like they hold me to a higher standard because I have more advantages to work with than Ethan did. They're not exactly perfectionists, but they don't give me a lot of room to make mistakes, either." The irony of Quinn's confession isn't lost on either of us. Through the veil of damp lashes covering his eyes, he glances down at me. "Wow, I guess being an asshole is genetic."

"Not any more than growing up in a bubble is."

He acknowledges my conviction-heavy statement by squeezing my hand. "You know, we don't have to talk about your family just because we talked about mine. I know it's not easy for you, so . . . whenever *you're* ready. I'm not going anywhere."

"Thanks," I say. "I promise I will someday . . . just not today. One family drama a day is my limit."

He laughs. "Okay then, why don't you fill me in on something a little less parental. What's going on with battle of the bands?"

The familiarity of a regular conversation with Quinn is like oxygen for my lungs. It feels good to breathe again.

I spend the next thirty minutes detailing exactly how it's possible that Gwen Stefani and Madonna have simultaneously ruined my life without ever having met me.

"It'll all work out," he says, when I finally come up for air. "If anybody can pull it off, it's you."

"What about you guys? I still don't know what your group is doing for the show."

"Sorry. You're going to have to wait for that one."

"That's not fair! I told you everything we're doing."

"You're just going to have to wait," he teases, flicking the end of my ponytail with his finger like he always does. "But you'll love it, I promise."

"Patience isn't my thing, Quinn."

"I'll take that into consideration for future activities," he says, as a sexy grin erupts across his face.

"Oh geez, just come here already." I wrap my arms around his neck and pull him in for a kiss.

"Oh my God," he mumbles against my lips. "We need to fight more often."

Smiling in agreement, my swollen ego forces me to ask, "Were you really jealous of Aidan?"

"Oh yeah," he says, leaning in for another kiss. "Wheelchair or not I was ready to kick his ass."

I laugh. "You should know the feeling was mutual. But be warned, if you so much as touch a hair on his head, I'll deck you myself."

TWENTY-ONE

One would think with all the commotion that wheelchairs and crutches create, two people walking into a room hand-in-hand would go unnoticed. It doesn't. From Fantine's ear-to-ear grin and Colin's fist pump, to Claire's glass-breaking rendition of that annoying *Titanic* song, we definitely don't make it into the mess hall unnoticed. Unfortunately, our arrival and obvious reunion isn't welcomed by everyone.

Despite his awareness of my feelings for Quinn, it comes as no surprise to see that Aidan looks a little heartbroken. He's rolled himself to the far corner of the room, and is having a hard time even looking at me. What *is* surprising is Rainbow's reaction. She's stopped dead in her tracks and glares at us like we just ran over her cat.

"What is her deal?" I whisper. "Are we breaking some counselor law or something?"

"No," Quinn whispers back. "I don't know what that's about. But whatever it is, I doubt she'll bring it up in front of everyone."

It's next to impossible to ignore Rainbow's laser beam glare, but within seconds of sitting down I find myself immersed in a debate over who is cuter, Hannah Montana or Miley Cyrus. Under different circumstances I would point out that they are, in fact, the same person and that there can't logically be room for dispute, but tonight I'm too distracted to care.

Rainbow's definitely got a bone to pick with me, and I intend to find out what it is.

* * *

"How is it possible you've never seen *Avatar*?" Fantine asks, sinking into her beanbag chair with a bowl of popcorn balanced on her lap. "It was like the most expensive movie ever made. It's amazing."

"I don't know, I just didn't," I say, unwilling to explain my rationale. (The truth is the blue people I saw in the previews freaked me out.)

Colin takes a handful of popcorn and shoves it into his mouth. "You'll love it, Cricket. It's got everything: action, adventure . . . *love!*"

Thankfully Quinn doesn't feel the need to try to convince me of the movie's worth; instead, he just stretches out his arm and invites me into that comfy spot beside him.

"You'll like it," he says. "It's a solid story line, decent acting, and there are no kids named Daniel-san."

"Very funny," I say, throwing him a jab to the side.

The movie begins and I settle in against him. Despite the desirable location, I can't seem to enjoy myself. All I can think about is how Rainbow hijacked our Saturday night Denny's outing. Fantine and the boys may have bought her whole, "it looks like it might rain, you should stay in and watch a movie instead," routine, but not me.

A lifetime later, when the world's longest movie finally comes to an end, Quinn and I set off hand in hand down the trail toward the cabins.

"You didn't watch any of it, did you?"

"What?" Quinn's question surprises me. I thought I'd faked my interest pretty well. "Of course I watched the movie. What do you think I was doing for the last three hours?"

"I'm pretty sure you were thinking about Rainbow."

My initial instinct is to tell him he's gone straitjacket—but he hasn't.

The only thing I remember of the billion-dollar movie was that the leading man, who happens to be in a wheelchair, was smoking hot and the blue chick with braids was even creepier than I thought she'd be. "This isn't how I imagined our late-night stroll through the woods would go down," I say. "Don't get me wrong, the moonlight's nice, but the conversation . . ."

"I don't want to talk about Rainbow any more than you do," he says. Giving my hand a deliberate tug, he pulls me against his chest, allowing his hands to settle naturally on my hips. "But it's obviously bugging you, so let's talk about it."

I look up at him but don't say anything.

He sighs. "Look, Rainbow's reaction at dinner was really bizarre, I'm not denying that. But I really don't think it means anything. She was probably just having a moment. And it's not like we're doing anything wrong. There's no rule against counselors being in a relationship."

Relationship? Could he be any cuter?

"Trust me," I say. "I want to believe that, but I really think there's more to it. Remember when I told you how she stares at me all the time?" He nods. "Okay, well, it's evolved into more than that. Now she says weird things to me. She makes personal references to things there's no way she should know."

"Like?"

I briefly consider telling him of my dislike for red meat, but after Fantine's response, decide that's not my best argument. "Yesterday she came by the mess hall when the girls and I were working on our set. She made a comment about knowing I was scared of heights and offered to climb the ladder to hang the decorations instead." As I hear the words pour out of my mouth, I realize this actually could be another meat situation. Thankfully, I see a thoughtful crinkle forming on his forehead. "And then on Thursday, when we were at the science shed and you had the kids look through the microscopes, she made a comment about how nicely the scar next to my eye had healed considering I had eleven stitches. I got those stitches when I was five, Quinn. How could she have known that?"

He turns my head to the side and surveys the scar in question. "I heard her say that," he says, grazing it with his thumb. "I did think it was a little weird that she mentioned it, but figured you must've told her about it."

"I didn't."

"Well, there's gotta be a logical explanation," he says. "Colin said that Rainbow has known your dad for a long time. That's the most obvious connection."

"That was my first thought, too," I say, relieved that he's taking me seriously. "But the more I think about it, the less likely it is. My dad's really private about our family life. Financial reporters are always trying to dig up something scandalous on him, so he works really hard at keeping personal matters quiet. We might not be BFFs, but there's no way he would keep a relationship with a woman from me my whole life. Not the kind of relationship that would warrant that kind of information being shared, anyway. He just wouldn't."

"Okay," he says, "If it's not your dad, then there's some other connection we're missing. . . ."

I am just about to respond, when the sound of stifled giggling interrupts my train of thought.

"Looks like we have an audience," he says, motioning over my shoulder.

I look behind me to a nearby tree where a beam of white light is streaking through the shadows. While our audience is savvy enough to stifle their giggles, they failed to choose a hideout wide enough to camouflage themselves. Claire's enormous pink night-gown is in plain view, as are both wheels of Meredith's wheelchair. No secret agent training here.

"I think I better go," I say, though I'm about ready to laugh.

"Yeah, I'd say so," he agrees, holding me against him in a part-ing hug. "I'll help you figure out what's going on with Rainbow. Whatever it is, you're entitled to know."

"Thanks, Quinn."

His arms release me and I turn to walk away.

"Wait," he says, taking my hand and pulling me back to him. "Shouldn't we give them something to talk about?"

Before I can even break a smile, he plants a tabloid-worthy kiss on my mouth. It's not until our visitors behind the tree break into hysterics that our lip lock is broken and my body returns to planet Earth.

"Good night, Cricket," he says, just a breath from my lips. "I'll see you in the morning. And good night to you, too, ladies," he calls, prompting a response of gasps and sniggers.

It takes me several deep breaths after Quinn leaves before I'm able to reorient myself.

"All right, you sneaks," I say, turning to face them. "Show your-selves."

There's a bit more laughter before Inspector Gadget and her four-wheeled sidekick finally appear from the darkness. Had I any doubt that Claire was the backbone of this botched operation before they came out of hiding it's quickly put to rest. Her cheeks are the color of a tomato and there's an, *Oh shit!* smirk plastered across her face.

"How long were you there and what did you hear?"

"Don't youuuu want to know what we saaaaw?"

"I know what you saw," I say, impressed with Meredith's comeback and total avoidance of my question. "What I asked was what did you *hear?*"

The girls exchange a wary glance before cautiously approaching me. "We had to go potty," Claire offers in an unnatural, subdued tone. "We didn't mean to spy on you. It just happened."

"Yeah," Meredith adds with a firm nod. "Thiiiiiings like that just haaaaappen sometimes."

"Oh yeah. I know," I say, still struggling to keep a straight face. "But you still didn't answer my question. Did you hear what we were talking about?"

"Oh no," Claire says. "We just watched. We didn't listen"

"Yeah. It's okay to looooook, you just caaaan't liiiisten."

"Right," I say. Not the best logic, but I'm willing to bet they're telling the truth. "Well, I think you two better hit the bathroom and get to bed. It's really late, and we've got a big day tomorrow. We're going to start in on the group rehearsals right after breakfast."

"Okay," Claire says, seconds before making a surprisingly swift movement toward me. Her meaty arms wrap around me, and she's squeezing me so tight I'm afraid my insides might break. "I love you, Cricket."

Now I can't breathe at all, and it's got nothing to do with Claire smashing me. It's like my heart has suddenly outgrown my chest. I return her hug, and quickly say, "Okay just . . . go to the bath-room."

The girls make their way up the hill, whispering about what they didn't hear but certainly saw, while I'm left to navigate my way through very unfamiliar territory. Did I just enjoy hugging Claire?

"Hey, Cricket," the hugger in question calls, her squishy face reappearing from the bathroom. "He's a good kisser, isn't he?"

I give an affirming nod.

"I knew it," she says, pumping her fist. "You can't look like that and be a bad kisser. Good night, Cricket!"

Good night, Claire.

TWENTY-TWO

Once again, I've pushed my morning primp time to the limit and am now hauling ass to catch up with the girls on their way to breakfast. I'm just rounding the last curve before the mess hall comes into sight, when Aidan rolls out from a small thicket of shrubs just ahead of me.

"Hey!" I say, slowly grinding my flip-flops to a stop. At first glance he looks like the same, all-American Aidan I've come to love, but as I approach him, I see something is drastically different. "Oh my God!" I shriek, and squat down to survey his swollen and very bruised left eye. "What happened?"

"Quinn," he says in a solemn voice.

"What! Quinn did this to you?"

He nods slowly, wincing as I run my finger across his bruise.

"Aidan . . ."

"Gotcha." He throws his head back, laughing. "I got nailed with a football last night."

"You little turd. That's not funny! I was about ready to give Quinn a beat down myself."

"You'd do that for me?" he says, offering a smile that would

177

make most girls weak in the knees.

"Well, I would have a minute ago, but now I'm not so sure. What are you doing out here? Doesn't Rainbow call the camp police if you're not at breakfast at seven sharp?"

"She pretty much lets me do my own thing. Besides, she's not here anyway."

"Where is she?"

"Pete said she had to run into town for something. I'm not really sure. But she's actually the reason I'm out here waiting for you."

"Okay . . ."

"Quinn and I were talking this morning—" He stops suddenly and looks at me with a serious face. "We're fine, by the way. Me and him. Nobody's going to kick anybody's ass."

"Well, that's a relief."

"Anyway, Quinn asked if you told me about what's going on with Rainbow. I told him you mentioned something the other day but never really filled me in on it—so he did." His smile slowly fades, as his blond brows cinch up in the center of his forehead. "Is it really bothering you as much as Quinn says?"

"At first it wasn't a problem until I would actually see her— that whole out of sight out of mind thing. But now . . . I don't know how to explain it. It's like she's got the inside track on me and I'm clueless as to how, or why, for that matter. If a relative stranger knew all kinds of personal stuff about you, wouldn't you want to know why?"

"Yes," he says without hesitation. "And that's exactly why Quinn and I have come up with a plan to figure it out."

❊ ❊ ❊

Breaking into Rainbow's private office in search of personnel files is hardly what I would consider a *plan*, but it's what my dreamy, future-engineer boyfriend and too-sweet, nonambulatory friend have come up with, so I guess we'll have to make it work.

While they're busy concocting their ridiculous scheme, I help clear the breakfast dishes and slide tables to the side of the room in preparation for my first group rehearsal.

Over the course of the last week, I've become perfectly comfortable with my two assigned campers and hardly notice when I'm responsible for all five girls. But with the boys added to the mix, I'm feeling a little anxious.

"Don't forget to have fun," Dr. Pete says quietly, passing through the room with a box of supplies in his arms.

Have fun. Right.

Heaving my deepest breath, I step forward. "All right, everybody, let's Vogue." As quickly as the words leave my mouth, James raises an oven-mitted hand into the air. "What?" I say.

"Wh-wh-what's a Vogue?"

"It's not a thing, James. It's a kind of dance."

"Liiike the ruuuumba?" Meredith says. "I know thaaaaat one. They dooooo it on *Daaancing with the Staaars*."

"It's nothing like the rumba," I say. At least I don't think it is. "It's more like—"

"The f-f-fox-trot?" James asks.

"No. They don't Vogue on *Dancing with the Stars*. It's something Madonna made up. It's just a series of slow, specific movements. Like you're unfolding yourself. How can you guys not know this? I thought you watched TV."

"It's like this," Claire says. And before I can beg her not to, she's belly down on the dirty floor, wriggling about like a sausage trying to work out of its casing.

"C-c-c-cool," James says.

"Soooo cooool," Meredith adds.

"No, it's not!" I try to act as a human shield and position myself between Claire and her very captive audience, but it's no use. She's moving surprisingly fast. "That's not cool at all," I say, pointing toward Claire with a grimace. "That's not how you Vogue. It's nothing like that."

Try as I might, my objections are lost among the cheers and taunts of, "Vogue! Vogue! Vogue!" that now fill the room.

"Ugh. You've got to be kidding me," I mutter, dragging a tired hand through my hair as I collapse into the nearest chair. "How the hell am I going to do this?"

Two hours later, I'm shuffling my way back to the bunkhouse, hunched over in pain.

"This is going to be such a train wreck," Fantine says.

I stop shuffling and look up to find her gawking at the campers ahead of us, each one doing their best Madonna-like moves. Despite the pain, I burst into another fit of laughter. Once we got past the whole Claire fiasco and they watched the "Vogue" video, things started to improve. But not by much. Witnessing their attempts to frame their faces and move their uncooperative bodies around like supermodels is probably the funniest thing I've ever seen.

"I told you!" I manage to say between laughs, gripping my side. "I had to watch that for two hours. Do you have any idea how sore my muscles are after laughing like this for two hours?"

"I'd have shit myself. I'm not kidding. That's just . . . just . . . ."

"Insane?"

"No," she says, a broad smile stretching across her face. "It's perfect. This is what it's all about. Having a good time. Not caring if you make a fool of yourself."

"Well, we've definitely got the fool part down. I have to go onstage with them—I'm freaking Madonna! Do you know how stupid I'm going to look?"

"Not as stupid as you're going to look when you're Gwen Stefani," she scoffs, raising a dark brow in my direction. I wish I could disagree with her but I can't. I *am* going to look stupid. "Oh, hey, Colin and Quinn told me about the plan. I think you're asking for trouble, Cricket."

"First off, it's not my plan," I say, wincing in pain as I straighten my posture. "They're the dumbasses who thought breaking into her office was the best way to get the information." She raises her brow again, but this time it's taking on an entirely different meaning. "I *do* have a right to know how she knows all this private stuff about me."

"Damn, girl. Relax. I'm not saying you don't have a right to know. I'm just saying that breaking and entering might not be the best approach. You could always just ask her. Did you ever think of that?"

"Of course," I say. "But after the way she treated me and Quinn yesterday, I think that bugging her about something she's obviously trying to keep secret would only piss her off more."

"Okay, there's some truth to that," she says. "But what about your dad? He's not saying anything either?"

"I haven't talked to him. Last I heard he was staying in Spain a few more days."

She holds my gaze long and hard. "Just make sure you're careful, okay? By some miracle you made it through the barf-o-rama without getting all of us fired. We don't need to tempt fate again."

"I know," I say. I know. . . .

TWENTY-THREE

"No way." I shake my head furiously. "There's no way in hell I'm doing that."

"Pleeeeeeease?"

I station my hands firmly on my hips, preparing for the ultimate showdown, but find myself melting like a stick of butter in the sun beneath Meredith's big doe-eyes.

"Ugh, fine," I concede, with little attempt to hide my annoyance. "I'll wear the stupid bra. But I swear, Meredith, you're going to owe me big. I want VIP seats at your next Olympic medal ceremony. Better seats than you give your own mother."

"Oh thaaaaank you, thaaank yoooooou!" she sings, spinning her neon chair in a circle. "You're going tooooo love it. I proooo-mise!"

Meredith wheels her way back to the wardrobe table, where Jamal, Colin's favorite camper, is needle and threading something shimmery, when Quinn strolls through the doorway with a smoldering grin on his face.

"Hey, how's rehearsal going?"

"It depends on who you ask. Considering I just agreed to wear a cone-shaped bra made entirely of black velvet and tongue depressors, I'd say it's going pretty bad. Meredith would say otherwise, though. What's up with you?"

"Rainbow's council meeting is set for tonight. Colin said he and Fantine would take the kids down to the lake after dinner so we can do what we need to do."

This is the night he's been planning for the last three days. The night Rainbow will be off-site at the Western Michigan Disabled Camping Association meeting for at least two hours, leaving her office unattended. The night I will finally learn the truth about her.

"Okay," I say. "And Aidan's on board for being the lookout?"

"Yep," he says coolly. "Everybody's good. It'll be perfect."

"I hope so."

"Wow!" a familiar screeching voice calls from the doorway. "You guys are working really hard in here, aren't you?"

With the subtlety of a hurricane, Rainbow tromps into the room, surveying the costumes and backdrops the kids are working on, while Quinn and I assume our newly adopted Rainbow-is-near position. We hold hands and prepare for public scrutiny.

"It looks like you're really taking ownership of this thing, Cricket," she says. "I take it you've decided on the final performance?"

For the past few days, Rainbow has said little more to either of us than one or two words at a time. Quinn notices this, too, and gives my hand a prompting tug.

"Uh . . . yeah," I say. "We're doing 'Vogue.'"

"Oh!" she says excitedly. "I love that song. I hope you borrowed a DVD from Sam. You know he knows everything about Madonna. He's like an encyclopedia."

"I did," I say skeptically. "And I downloaded a few things onto my phone . . . but I'm still not sure it was the best idea."

"Well, I think it's a great idea," she says, laying her speckled hand on my shoulder like it's a natural occurrence. I have to force myself not to scream. "And I'm sure all the parents are going to love it. Right, Quinn?"

"Definitely," he says, all chill and unflustered. "From what I hear, all the kids think it's cool—even the boys, which is saying a lot. I'm not sure I would've been up for a Madonna stage act when I was fifteen."

"Well, the world will never know." She laughs, finally removing her clammy hand from me. "Well, I better leave you guys to it. I've got a ton on my to-do list to get ready for the parents on Saturday night. We want to make sure everything runs without a hitch, don't we?"

I nod, completely dumbstruck, while Quinn offers another bullshit response about the sanctity of maintaining punctuality. Rainbow laughs like a hyena again, before turning on her worn sneakers and heading out into the afternoon heat.

"What the hell was that?"

"I have no idea," he says. "She was like a totally different person. Maybe she's got an evil twin locked in her office and the real Rainbow only gets to come out under a full moon."

"That would explain a few things," I say. "But I think we would have known it wasn't really her. In the movies, the evil twin is always the hot sexy one."

"The one who wears a tongue-depressor bra?"

"Exactly," I say. "So you really think we're good to go tonight?"

"Yeah, we're good. Colin says these meetings run like clock-work. They start at six-thirty and rarely end before eight. We've got a solid two-hour block from the time she leaves until the meeting ends. I don't think we're going to be in there more than half an hour anyway."

"We need to plan on that. If we can't get in and out in thirty minutes—we're just asking for it."

"Agreed. But it's nice to have a cushion if we need it."

"And what are we going to do about Pete?" I say. "If Pete finds out, you know he'll tell Rainbow. He's a cool guy and all, but he's going to be a doctor. There's probably some oath he has to take about telling the authorities if he witnesses a crime being commit-ted."

"Pete's going to the meeting, too. He's leading CPR training or something."

"Okay. What about Sam?"

"Sam always watches movies in his trailer after dinner. Aidan will camp out right under that willow tree behind the mess hall—

he'll be able to keep an eye on the office and Sam."

"Okay," I say. "I guess you've got it all covered then, don't you?"

"Pretty much. I did earn a scholarship, you know? There's a lot more going on here than just this pretty face."

"Oh yeah," I say, blushing. "I'm very aware of that."

TWENTY-FOUR

After dinner we assemble the kids for their evening of night fishing and lakeside s'mores. Everyone's thrilled with the plan, except James. Apparently his ideal nighttime activities have less to do with fishing poles and more with his oven-mitted hand traveling under Claire's shirt. Shame, shame, James.

"All right, everybody," Colin addresses the campers in his booming voice. "Follow the path carefully. There are a lot of gaps in the asphalt and a few loose rocks along the way. For those of you in chairs, *please* take it slowly. We know you're hell on wheels, but you don't need to prove it tonight."

With their poles, bait, graham crackers, marshmallows, melting Hershey's bars, sweatshirts, and cans of bug spray in hand, the kids follow along behind Fantine while Colin takes up the rear. No one seems to notice that the three of us are hanging back, allowing the parade of the hobbled, wheeled, and wonky-eyed to proceed without us.

"You ready?" Aidan says, when Colin's head finally disappears out of sight.

"Yep," says Quinn. "Are you, Crick?"

I look over my shoulder for the fifteenth time, confirming that the old pickup is officially off the premises before I answer. "I guess so," I finally say.

"Sweet," Aidan says. "Let's get this over with so I can get my s'mores on. I've already checked in on Sam. He's about a half hour into the first *Lord of the Rings*. He'll be good for the rest of the night."

Aidan is way too eager for my liking. He's practically floating with excitement as he wheels his way up the path toward the small, two-room building that hosts Rainbow's cabin and the camp office.

"Don't worry," Quinn says as we trail along behind. "She won't have a clue we've been here. We'll be just like the Domino's pizza guy—thirty minutes or less."

"Except the pizza guy doesn't get thrown into jail if he's late."

"Nobody's going to jail," he says, smiling. "But I bet you would look hot in an orange jumpsuit."

I roll my eyes. "Idiot."

Aidan assumes his position under the willow tree, while Quinn carefully opens the weathered rear door of the office. As I tiptoe across the warped planks of the tiny porch and step inside the small, dark space, it dawns on me that my anxiety about this quest has less to do with getting caught and everything to do with what I might find.

Being the braver party in our dynamic duo, Quinn heads straight for the two-drawer steel filing cabinet on the far side of the room, while I take the less obtrusive route—perusing through the small stacks of mail on her desk.

The first stack produces nothing more than a few invoices for medical supplies, a past due Verizon bill, and random credit card offers, and the second even less exciting. There are two envelopes; one is addressed to Mom and has an Edward Cullen return address label in the corner (nice penmanship, Claire), and the other has a little cutout window for an address to show though. The American Electric Power Company will be getting paid this month.

"Anything?"

"Nada." I look up from where I'm carefully restacking the mail, and find him head deep in a drawer. "What about you?" I ask. "Did you find something?"

"Nah." He sighs and slams the drawer shut. "It's just a lot of random crap from her college days, which is sort of surprising considering how organized she is. Hopefully this other drawer's a little more encouraging." He fumbles for a moment with the tiny switch lock on the front of the door before it finally springs open. "Got it," he says.

"What's in there?"

"The mother lode," he says proudly. "Personnel files."

I hurry around the desk and kneel down on the floor beside him.

"Colin Aceti, Analeise Dummel, David Early . . . Wow, a lot of people have worked here," he mumbles, thumbing his way through the sea of confidential information. "Fantine Marquez, Rochelle

Mendler . . . Ah, here we go. Constance Montgomery." He pulls a thin manila folder from the stack. Over his shoulder he asks, "You ready for this?"

"Yes," I say. "Open it."

"Okay, here goes nothing." He flips it open and begins to read. "Constance Elaine Montgomery, nickname: Cricket. Date of birth, September seventh. Hey"—he pauses and glances back at me—"you're turning the big one eight next month."

I nod.

"Good to know," he says, before turning back to the folder. "Lives on Astor Street . . . Chicago . . . attends Parker Prep Academy . . ." He flips to a second sheet and scans the document like a doctor does before he asks you what's wrong. "There's not much here," he finally says. "It's all the basics about you, but it's almost like something is missing. . . ."

He begins fingering through the remaining folders before finally pulling the very last file from the drawer. Over his shoulder I see the label: Quinn Youngsma.

"You see how my file has all this extra stuff on the right side?"

I creep closer, and watch as he flips through the stack of papers fastened to the right side of the folder. There are handwritten notes, a newspaper clipping with a picture of him in a soccer uniform, and a report of some kind.

"What is that?" I ask, pointing to the report.

"We had to submit a formal writing sample with our

applications before we were ever considered for employment," he says, thumbing page by page through the report that's easily twenty pages long. The only thing I've ever written that was twenty pages long was my Christmas list. "God," he says, "I couldn't write for shit in high school . . . this is pathetic. Good thing I'm not an English major. Did you have to submit a writing sample?"

"No. I didn't do anything," I say. "One minute I was trying to get stoned, and the next minute I was here. I was practically kidnapped."

"Hold on." He sets the folder down and repositions himself so he's facing me. "What do you mean you were *trying* to get stoned?"

"It's a long story," I say, which is a total lie. The story isn't long, it's just monumentally embarrassing.

"Well then, I guess you better get to explaining since we've got less than twenty minutes left on our timer."

I don't want to get into this right now (or ever), but I know Quinn, and he's not about to let me off the hook without some kind of response. "Ugh, fine. Let's just say that pot and oregano look really similar to an untrained eye."

His eyes grow wide and his body begins to shake with silent laughter.

"This is why I didn't want to tell you. I knew you'd make fun of me."

"Well, yeah," he says, laughing hard now. "How can you *not* know the difference? You are such a dork."

"I'm not a dork!" I protest. "It was mortifying! The guys with us were in college. We were trying to impress them."

"Did it work?"

"What do you think?"

It takes him a minute to compose himself. "In your case, I think being a dork is underrated."

"Well, you would know," I say with a smirk. "Now can we please move past my Bob Marley moment and figure this out? It's weird that I don't have any extra stuff in my file, right?"

"Yes and no. It's only weird because the rest of us had to jump through crazy hoops to work here. It makes sense that you don't have anything else in your file—"

"Wait a second!" I silence him with a smack to the shoulder. "What did you say was in that top drawer?"

"Just a bunch of old crap. What are you looking at?" He rises to his feet and joins me in staring at the framed diploma on the wall. Ironically, it's hanging right next to the plaque donated in memory of my mom. "I didn't realize Rainbow went to DePaul."

"Me, either," I say. "It says she graduated in ninety-one."

"Okay . . ."

My heart starts beating a little faster. "My mom graduated from DePaul in ninety-one, too."

Before I can even ask, Quinn is back at the filing cabinet searching through the top drawer again. "Here," he says, handing me the first of two, three-inch-wide hanging folders he's yanked out. "Since we're pressed for time, it's probably better to have both of us looking."

I rest my butt up against the edge of Rainbow's desk and begin sorting through the file. After just a few minutes, I can tell it contains exactly what Quinn said it did—crap. There are about a hundred alumni pledge cards, an old DePaul campus directory, a pale yellow Post-it with a phone number scribbled in blue ink, a gas station receipt—"

"Holy crap."

"What?" I say, dropping the Exxon receipt without a second thought. "Did you find something?" He slowly turns to face me. His wide eyes make me nervous.

"You look just like her."

He holds my gaze for a beat before handing me a photograph. Despite their matching graduation caps and gowns, I recognize both of the smiling faces the instant my eyes land on them. The one on the right is a younger version of the freckled, redheaded woman I've come to hate. The other is the green-eyed beauty I don't remember but miss every day. Mom.

Without warning, my chest tightens, and I feel the unwelcome arrival of that burning, aching pain in my throat; the one that always come right before I cry. I slouch farther against the desk's edge, staring at the picture until the image grows blurry.

"Even Rainbow gets to have memories of her?" I say in a near whisper.

"What?"

"Why does everybody get a piece of her but me? My whole life I've wanted to know who she was," I say, choking on words I never imagined I'd be saying. "Something beyond the cookie-cutter rhetoric they print on fundraising programs. But nobody tells me anything. I ask . . . but they won't tell me. And now . . . now even *she* gets to have memories of her?"

Sympathy fills Quinn's face as he pulls me tight against his chest.

"Cricket, I'm sorry," he says, and he presses his lips on my head. "He probably didn't mean to hurt you. Maybe he just thought he was protecting you. But you're right, he had no right to keep her from you."

Quinn's soothing words are like a balm to my aching heart, and the longer he repeats them, the more I'm assured that for the first time in my life, someone actually understands my loss. It's not about the death of a mother, but rather the complete absence of her memory. And if anyone understands how precious a memory can be, it's Quinn.

"I do actually have one memory of her," I say a few minutes later, when my tears have stopped.

He pushes away from me so he can see my face. "Oh yeah?"

"She used to carry those big pink peppermints in her purse. You know the kind you get at the drugstore that fall apart as you put it in your mouth? Of all the memories to have of your mother, right?"

"They're hot pink and about this big?" He raises his hand and makes a little circle with his fingers. "I love those. My nana always has a big jar full of them on her kitchen counter."

The shared pleasure over the ninety-nine-cent treats make me smile, and for a moment I forget that I'm in the middle of committing my first felony.

TWENTY-FIVE

Bam! Bam! Bam!

The pounding on the door jars us both from our emotionally charged moment back to reality.

"They're here!" The panic in Aidan's voice carries through the crack beneath the door, prompting Quinn to release me so fast, I really should be wearing a seat belt. "You guys, come on!"

We both survey the damage in the room. It looks like a tornado passed through.

"Go with him," Quinn says. "I'll take care of this."

"No way, it's my mess. I'm not letting you clean it up alone."

Whack! The door flings open, banging into the wall behind it. Heart racing, I turn over my shoulder and am relieved to find Aidan in the doorway, though I have no idea how he managed to get himself up there.

"Hurry the hell up!" he says. "I can see the dust cloud coming in from up the road. They're gonna be here any minute!"

"Cricket, *go!*" Quinn stops reloading the file drawer so he can look me square in the eye. "It'll be a lot easier for one person to get out of here unseen than three. Just go with him—I'll be right behind you."

"Are you sure?"

"*Yes!* Now get out of here!"

Against my better judgment, I turn and clear the small distance to the door in a matter of seconds. Aidan is waiting with one hand on the doorknob, and an intense look on his face. A vision of Edward ordering me into the protection of Jacob's hairy wolf arms before the Volturi arrive suddenly flashes through my mind and I shudder. Claire's got way too much influence on me.

"Let's roll," he says. He gives the door a hearty tug and wheelies himself to the ground. I skip both steps, landing with a *thud*, and immediately take off after him.

We fast-track it behind the mess hall and past Sam's trailer. Aidan's arms are working overtime, spinning so fast they're blurring like blades on a propeller. Despite my flip-flops, I manage to hang just a few feet behind him, although with the way my heart is pumping, I doubt that will last for long.

The distinct sound of tires on gravel prompts Aidan to curse, and me to dig a little deeper into an energy reserve I didn't know I had.

"We're almost there!" he shouts.

Following his lead, I scramble up and over a small embankment, and into a thicket of white pine trees just behind the flagpole. Aidan skids to a dusty halt while I stumble in beside him, immediately squatting down to his level and out of sight.

"You okay?"

"I don't know." I gasp and clutch my chest. "I think I'm going to need a paramedic. Or an inhaler."

"Oh, the burden of having legs."

"Ah shit, Aidan," I say, still gasping. "I'm sorry, I didn't mean—"

"Relax," he says, trying to catch his own breath. "I'm just kidding."

"You're an ass," I say, trying to ignore the collection of fresh scrapes and scratches on my feet. The overwhelming scent of pine has my stomach turning, so I do my best to focus my attention on the little two-room cabin we've just escaped.

"What do you think will happen if he gets caught?"

"He's not going to get caught."

"*If* he does." I turn to him with desperation in my voice. "What would happen? Would she fire him?"

"Probably."

"What about school? Do you think she could get his scholarship taken away? His parents can't afford the tuition."

"I don't know."

"Oh God!" My hands cover my mouth as a horrific idea crosses my mind. "Do you think she'd have him arrested? For trespassing or breaking and entering? I know we were joking about it before, but this is real, Aidan. Like *real*. He could go to jail or stand trial—"

"Cricket," he says, obviously annoyed. "Nothing's going to happen to him."

"What makes you so sure? You've seen how up and down Rainbow's been with us. For all we know, she might have him duct-taped to a chair right now."

"*Dude*," he says, looking at me with the eyes of an exhausted parent. "He's fine, okay? Nothing's going to happen to Quinn. He's not going to jail, or detention, or anywhere in between."

"How can you be so sure?"

"Because"—he motions his head to the side—"he's already out."

"What?" I turn back toward the office and see Quinn tearing through the field we've just crossed. His cheeks are pink, and his eyes are wide. "Oh, thank God!" I get to my feet and begin waving my arms above my head.

"So much for staying hidden," Aidan mumbles.

The second Quinn spots me, I instantly feel relieved. With the cloud of dust he's kicking up, it's nearly impossible to see if anyone's following him, but based on his enthusiasm, I'm guessing we're safe. He clears the embankment in one enormous, Spider-Man-like leap, landing with his hands on the ground.

"Holy crap!" He collapses against me, completely out of breath. "I've never run so fast in my life."

"Did she see you?" I ask.

"No," he says, breathing hard. "At least I don't think so. I thought for sure I was screwed. Right after you guys left, I heard the truck pull up, and the car doors shut, but no one ever came into the office. I ended up just shoving the rest of the paperwork into the drawer so I could get the hell out of there. Hopefully she won't go digging around for old pictures anytime soon."

"So you guys actually found something?"

Quinn and I exchange a quick glance before I answer.

"It turns out Rainbow and my mom were friends in college. I'm not sure how close they were, but based on the picture we found, I'm guessing BFF territory."

"Really?" Aidan's eyes widen. "Well, that blows my whole secret mommy theory."

I feel my brows tighten together. "Your secret mommy theory?"

"Yeah. I started thinking you'd find an original birth certificate that proved Rainbow was actually your mom. Like she took off when you were a baby and your dad just concocted the whole cancer story to protect you or something."

"Are you high?"

He laughs. "It wasn't that far-fetched an idea, was it?" He looks to Quinn who just shrugs.

"You both watch way too much *Maury*. Anybody can tell by looking at us that we're not related." Quinn shrugs again, though this time it's in my favor. Now that he's seen the photographic evidence it's hard to refute. "But that's beside the point," I say. "We still don't know who's leaking all my personal info to Rainbow."

"What are you talking about?" Aidan says. "It's obviously your dad."

"It doesn't add up," I say, shaking my head. "My dad is really private when it comes to me. There's no way he'd share my personal information with someone I've never even met." Unless he was already friends with Rainbow, too. "Oh my God." I recoil slightly at my sudden light bulb moment. "If Mom and Rainbow were *that* close, maybe my dad knows her, too."

"He does donate money here," Quinn says. "It's definitely a possibility."

Nodding, Aidan chimes in. "Yeah, maybe she just provided moral support. In the dark, without any clothes on—"

"Aidan, *stop*!" I kick the wheel of his chair with my foot. "Any more of those images and I'm going to have to give myself a lobotomy."

"Okay, okay," he says. "But seriously, maybe she helped with things around the house or was a shoulder to cry on. You were really young—there's no way you'd remember."

I shake my head. "Carolyn was the only one. She's told me before—he wouldn't talk to anybody else but her—" Hard and fast, the memory of Rainbow questioning Sean about Carolyn's absence when I arrived strikes me down like a bolt of lightning.

No way.

Carolyn is the leak?

TWENTY-SIX

I waaaaaas thinking I could do a haaaaandstand and then Cricket could pop up in betweeeen my legs. Don't you think thaaaat would be coooool?"

I'm not sure why it surprises me that Claire would agree that my head suddenly appearing from between Meredith's useless legs would be a good addition to our train wreck of a routine, but it does. "That's ridiculous," I say. "And gross. People don't want to see my head popping out of your crotch!"

Claire bursts into laughter while Meredith covers her blushing cheeks with her hands.

"It's perfoooormance art, Cricket. Open to interp-in-int-terp . . ."

"Interpretation," I say. "But it doesn't matter. It's going to look stupid. I'm not doing it."

"Whaaaaat is your problem, Cricket?"

"Excuse me?" I stare down at Meredith. "What did you say?"

"Yooooou heard me," she says, unmoved by my tone. "You are reeeeally grumpy tooooday."

"Yeah. You're bitchy," Claire adds. Heaven forbid any

conversation pass by without input from her. "Is it about this morning? Or do you need more Midol?"

"No, Claire," I say, my eyes practically rolling out of their sockets. "As I've said before I *don't* need any Midol. I'm sorry I'm being bitchy; I'm just upset about something that happened last night." And can't stop thinking about it. "What happened this morning?"

"The thiiiiing with Quinn," Meredith says.

A chill races up my spine. "What thing with Quinn?"

"With Raaaainbow and what heeeee did."

"What are you talking about?" I jump to my feet, losing what little patience I had. Meredith jerks back. "I'm sorry," I say, aware I probably look like a blonde Godzilla from her angle. "I'm not trying to scare you, but I need to know exactly what happened. Where's Quinn?"

I see a lump pass down her throat as she swallows back what's bound to be an eruption of tears.

"He . . . uh . . . Raaaainbow said . . ."

"Rainbow said she needed to talk to Quinn. In her office."

I whip my head over my shoulder to face Claire. Finally she has something useful to say.

"Did she say why?"

She shrugs. "Not really. They left so Colin had to finish collecting rocks with us. I found a white one. It looks like a diamond, want to see?"

"Not now!" I say.

Shirking my counselor responsibilities, I bolt through the mess hall and out the front doors like my ass is on fire. There is no way she's going to take him down for anything that happened last night!

Ignoring my screaming hamstrings, I sprint across the small field that separates the two buildings, and come to a screeching halt just feet from Rainbow's office.

"Oh, shit," I mutter, my already labored breath catching in my throat. What is he doing here?

With one hand on my side holding back an impending cramp, I slowly make my way toward the sleek silver sedan that's resting beside the beater camp truck. The country club parking sticker on the windshield, and the ever-present Starbucks cup in the center console are confirmation that my dad is in fact on-site, and not in Spain where he is supposed to be.

I should be terrified by my discovery, but I'm too worried about Quinn to care. I stomp across the front porch and fling the office door open. Rainbow is the first person I see. She's sitting behind her desk with an intense look on her face that slowly fades to confusion when she sees me.

"Cricket . . . what are you doing here?" she asks, standing up slowly while keeping her hands firmly planted on the desk in front of her.

I ignore her question and turn to Quinn, who's sitting in the sad excuse for a guest chair to my left. "Are you okay?" I ask.

He nods, though the quick shift of his eyes tells a different story.

I look over my right shoulder and find my dad standing in the corner of the room. To some, his face would be unreadable. But to me, it's crystal clear.

"Why are you here?" I ask cautiously, aware that the last time I saw him look this pissed was the day before he sent me here. "I thought you had to stay in Spain."

"I got back a few hours ago. Rainbow had me summoned the minute we touched down at O'Hare."

"Oh," I say, hoping that some of his anger may stem from jet lag. The tension in the room is so thick it's hard to breathe. "Well . . . uh . . . why did she call you?" I say.

He continues to hold my gaze with the same intensity that has made him one of the Midwest's most successful businessmen, before his expression softens. Just a smidge.

"We need to talk." He unfolds his arms from his chest, and motions to the empty folding chair beside him. "And you don't need to be here."

Heart threatening to beat out of my chest, I go sit down without comment as Quinn takes the not-so-subtle cue. His solemn expression leaves me with no indication as to what's been going on. He leaves without a word.

"We need discuss what went on here last night," Rainbow says, the second the door closes.

"What do you mean?"

"Come on, Cricket." My dad sounds exhausted as he makes his

way to the other side of the room, dropping into the chair Quinn just vacated. "Breaking and entering is a serious offense. Just confirm what your friend has been telling us so we can move on and get you home."

Not too long ago I would have traded my left arm to hear those words come from his mouth, but now they leave me feeling nauseous. There's no way I'm leaving—not now. I swallow back the sour taste welling in the back of my throat and say, "What exactly did Quinn tell you?"

He leans forward in the chair, dropping that same Exxon receipt I held last night on Rainbow's desk, before resting his forearms on his knees. *Shit!* I never put it back in the drawer. "He said he was trying to help you track down some information you were looking for, and thought that Rainbow's private office was a logical place to start. He said you had absolutely no idea what he was up to, and all responsibility should be placed on him. Is that true?"

I nearly lose my breath, as a dangerous combination of heartache and gratitude threatens to take over.

"*Well?*" he says, his patience running dangerously thin.

The old Cricket would have answered yes without batting an eyelash. When it comes to the art of parental BSing, I am the master. And my poor father is virtually incapable of distinguishing a lie from the truth when it comes to me. But as his question bounces around in my head and the parting image of Quinn is still fresh in my mind, I can't even imagine lying.

"No. It's not."

"What do you mean?" he says sharply. "Which part isn't true?"

I have to swallow hard again before I can answer. "It's true that Quinn was in here because I was looking for something. But he wasn't alone." I see my dad's jaw tighten as he braces for the words he knows I'm about to say. "I was here, too."

"Oh, for God's sake, Cricket—"

"What exactly were you looking for?" Rainbow asks.

I know I should answer her, but I can't speak. And forget about knowing where to look—my dad is like a volcano ready to erupt and Rainbow has this vacant expression on her face.

"Dammit, Constance," Dad says in a tone I've never heard before. "Answer her!"

"I . . ."

"What?" Rainbow prods. "What is it?"

Clueless as to how to broach the subject, I pull the photo I stole the night before from my back pocket, and with a shaky hand lay it down on the desk in front of her, right next to the receipt. "I know you've been talking to Carolyn," I say, hedging all my bets on one bold assumption.

Her jaw nearly drops and her already pale complexion manages to fade a few more shades. Assumption confirmed. "Oh dear," she mutters.

"What is she talking about?" Dad says, interrupting Rainbow's reality check. "What about you and Carolyn?" His question hangs in the air like a foul odor, when the image of his young wife finally catches his eye. He stares at it for a moment before snatching it from her desk. "Where did you get this?" He faces me, raising the photo in the air.

"From a drawer in Rainbow's office," I say nervously, shifting my attention back and forth between the two of them. "That's why we broke in. You knew things about me, personal things, and I wanted to know why . . . and who was telling you."

Rainbow nods her head. "Of course you did," she says. "Of course you'd want to know. You have every right to."

"Wait a minute," Dad says. "Carolyn's been feeding you information about Cricket? Why the hell would she do that?"

"Because Connie asked her to," she says, unaffected by his obvious contempt for her. "She knew you would never do it, so before she passed she asked Carolyn to keep me up-to-date on Cricket. It was something she did in private—you never knew."

"That's ridiculous! Carolyn's worked for me for twenty years. She'd never betray me like that."

"It's not a betrayal to her, Burt. She was honoring Connie's wishes—"

"Stop!" It's my turn to play catch up. I turn to face Dad. "Why wouldn't you have stayed in touch with her if that's something Mom wanted?"

He doesn't answer me. He just stares at me with a cold, distant look in his eye.

"Because your father and I don't get along very well," Rainbow answers for him in a somber voice. "He thinks running a successful company is more important than spending time with your wife and child."

"Oh, for the love of God," he says. "Are we really going to start up this nonsense again? Connie moved on with her life and you couldn't accept that. It's the same story it was twenty years ago."

"Your mom was an incredible woman," Rainbow says to me, completely ignoring Dad's bold accusations. "She was my best friend and one of the smartest, funniest people I've ever known. I'll admit it was hard to watch her run off and get married only six months after meeting your dad, but it wasn't because I couldn't accept it." She glares at my dad. "It was because over the course of their marriage your mother changed—her enthusiasm for life just fizzled out."

"This is nonsense—"

"*No, Burt*, it's not," Rainbow cuts him off. "What you may not know, or may not want to face, is that Connie felt desperately alone before she died. Yes, she had this beautiful little girl"—she motions to me—"and all the things that money could buy, but you weren't there. And you"—she turns back to me—"you have every right to be angry with me, but I want you to understand that being part of your life, if only through pictures and e-mails, has been the best gift that your mother could have given me. When you stepped out of the car that first day . . . my God"—she bites her lip, failing to hide her emotions—"it was like looking at my freshman roommate for the first time again. I just wanted to take you in my arms and squeeze you—but I knew I couldn't, because you didn't know me. And as much as I wanted to tell you, part of the arrangement with you being here was that I not say I had any connection to you or your mom."

"Then why would you even send me here?" I say, looking to my dad for an answer. He just looks at me—his jaw still clinched like a vice. "Dad?"

"Your mom added a rider to her will just before she passed," Rainbow says, since my father is apparently incapable of speech. "Not only did she leave a percentage of her personal inheritance from your grandparents' estate to the camp, but she also specified that she wanted you to spend a summer working here some time before you turned eighteen." She glances in his direction. "Considering she'll be eighteen in a few weeks, I'd say you held out as long as you could."

"Wait a minute." I stand up, even more confused than I was a minute ago. "You were going to send me here anyway? This had nothing to do with the country club thing?"

"Actually, no," he says. His voice is so cold it gives me chills. "I hadn't planned on sending you here at all. But you were spiraling out of control at home, and I didn't know what else to do with you. Sending you to Hawaii with your best friend didn't seem like the best solution to your unacceptable behavior. Not that it's improved much since you've been here." He turns back to Rainbow with a disgusted look on his face. "Obviously your assurance that she'd be surrounded by responsible young adults this summer wasn't accurate. She went from smoking oregano to breaking and entering. What kind of delinquents do you have on staff here?"

"Quinn is not a delinquent!" I say, leaping out of my seat. "Don't you dare call him that! The only reason he even got involved with this is because he cares about me and knew how upset I was. Quinn is amazing and smart and funny and the most honest person I've ever met—and I love him!"

He blows out a heavy sigh. "Are we really going to get wrapped up in a teenage love affair now? Just because some boy you've known a couple of weeks is willing to take the heat for you, doesn't mean you're in love."

My eyes begin to burn, and that painful ache is back in my throat. I want to take a deep breath, but I can't. From the corner of my eye, I see Rainbow's hands balled up into fists, and then it hits me. That's why she acted the way she did when she saw me with Quinn.

"Oh my God," I turn to her. "You were afraid I was going to do exactly what my mom did, weren't you? That night at dinner, when you saw us together for the first time. You thought I was getting too invested in a guy—in Quinn."

She holds my gaze for a moment before her eyes fall to the desk. "I suppose I'm a little protective of you, even though I have no right," she says. "It was wrong of me to pass my own anxieties on to you, and I'm sorry for that. You're right about Quinn. He's a bright kid with a good head on his shoulders, who obviously cares a great deal for you."

"He won't be punished for this, will he?"

She shakes her head. "Of course not."

I feel the tiniest bit of relief, like maybe the whole world is not about to come crashing down, until my dad says, "Go pack your stuff."

"What?"

"I said get your stuff. I'm taking you home."

"No, I can't go home. Battle of the bands is in two days! We've been working our asses off. Everyone needs me to be here!"

"Please, Burt," Rainbow adds in a surprisingly calm voice. "The kids have been working so hard on this. They'd be devastated if she wasn't here until the end."

"It's not going to happen," he says with a voice devoid of any emotion. "I went against my better judgment allowing her to come up here this summer, trusting this place would provide a good environment for her to see what life was really about. Clearly that didn't happen."

"Dad, please! Don't make me leave. You don't understand. I *have* changed. I'm so much different than I was when I got here. I've made friends with the other counselors. And the kids . . . these kids are really cool—"

"*Constance*. The decision has been made. Go get your things and meet me in the car."

I can actually feel my heart breaking inside my chest. Like a million tiny daggers ripping through me at the same time. "You're such an asshole!" I try to scream, but my voice is raw and tired and comes out more like a puppy's yelp. "Don't you get it? You're not punishing me because I broke into her office; you're doing it because you were a lousy husband and father and you can't own up to it!"

I storm out of the office and into the blinding afternoon sun. The sudden transition from chaos to calm is almost unbearable.

"Hey!"

I turn to my right and see Quinn running toward me. The concerned look on his face breaks my heart all over again—and then I start to cry.

"He's making me leave," I manage to say, before collapsing against his chest. "He . . . he told me to go pack my stuff and get in the car. He doesn't even care that we've got the show, or about the kids, or you. . . ."

I realize now I must be rambling again because Quinn keeps stroking my hair saying, "It's going to be okay." I finally settle down enough to take a deep breath, though it only helps for a second. I feel like I've been sucker punched by Mike Tyson. And poor Quinn. How many days in a row does he have to play therapist to a wounded Cricket? "Tell me what happened," he says.

Through more tears and a barrage of incoherent words, I manage to unload the details of the conversation. I tell him every ugly, painful morsel, and my face is buried in his shirt the whole time.

"What do you want me to do?" he asks, leaning down to look at me. "Do you want me to talk to him? Maybe I can convince him to change his mind."

I feel another pang when I see that his eyes are red and puffy, too.

"Cricket," my dad's booming voice interrupts us from behind. "Go get your stuff. I want a minute with your . . . *friend*."

"It's okay," Quinn says before I have a chance to object. "We'll work it all out. It's probably better to just do what he says right now."

"You want me to pack my stuff?"

"It'll be okay. I promise."

I look at him, trying to trust what he's saying, but I'm scared out of my mind. What if this doesn't work? What if I really have to leave?

"Okay," I finally agree. "I'll be back in a few minutes. But please don't let him get to you. He's mean and unreasonable when he's mad."

"Don't worry about me," he says stoically. "I'm a pro with difficult parents. I'll see you in a minute."

✳ ✳ ✳

My head is throbbing and my stomach is in a knot by the time I make my way across camp and into the empty bunkhouse I've called home for the last thirteen days. In a million years I never would have thought I'd be sad to leave this dirty hole-in-the-wall, but as I slide back the plastic curtain and peer at the two empty beds, I find myself holding back another wave of emotion. *How could my dad do this to me?*

I shove all my things into my duffel without caring what's clean or dirty, hoping I'll be back within the hour to unload it all again. I hook the strap over my shoulder, dropping a quickly scribbled note on Fantine's bed with my cell number and e-mail address, and walk through the main cabin with my head down. Just one glimpse of that ridiculous Hannah Montana throw pillow on Meredith's bed, I'll be so far over the edge of emotional breakdown there will be no turning back.

I step out onto the porch and tug the door shut behind me. The feeling that washes over me is awful and makes me feel sick all over again. I'm not sure how I know, but I just do. I'm not coming back.

Rainbow and Quinn are waiting for me at the top of the hill when I return a while later. The looks on their faces tell the story I don't want to hear.

"Cricket," Rainbow says, approaching me slowly. "Can I have a minute?"

Quinn offers a faint smile before stepping back to allow us privacy.

"I loved your mom very much," she says earnestly. "It was a

painful decision when I decided not to see her anymore, but I found myself growing more and more resentful of your dad, and it just wasn't healthy for any of us. I didn't even know you existed until a few days before she passed. She called me and we talked for hours . . .crying, reminiscing, catching up on each other's lives—" She pauses to clear her throat before propping her sunglasses on the top of her head. Her eyes are as puffy and bloodshot as mine. "I am so sorry that I didn't tell you the moment you arrived, and I don't blame you if you hate me—"

"I don't hate you," I say abruptly, surprising us both. "But I don't know you. And you don't know me . . . not really anyway."

She nods. "You're right. I don't know you at all, but if you give me chance, I'd like to."

I stare up at the strange, pasty-faced woman who is so desperate to be part of my life. I'd never choose to be friends with someone like her, or even stand in line behind at the movies, but she claims to care about me. And for some reason I believe her.

"I'll think about it," I say, which is all I can give her right now.

"That's good enough for me. And for what it's worth"—she lays a gentle hand on my shoulder—"I think you did a hell of a job here. I'd welcome you back as a counselor anytime."

I can't help but chuckle. "I bet you never thought you'd be saying that."

She smiles.

"I guess I'll think about that, too," I say.

She gives my shoulder a parting squeeze before she walks away in silence. Under different circumstances, I'd be thrilled for the private time Quinn and I have just been granted, but right now it feels like I'm staring down the barrel of a loaded gun.

"Did that go okay?" he asks, walking toward me wearing an expression that makes me nervous.

I slump my shoulders and let my bag fall to the ground. "As well as it could, I guess. She said I could come back to work next summer if I wanted."

"Is that something you want?"

"If you're going to be here."

His expression slowly morphs back into the warm, genuine one I've come to know and love, and suddenly the thought of not seeing it tomorrow is too much to handle. I turn away from him.

"I'll be back in Chicago soon," he says, taking my hands in his. "School starts in a few weeks. But the thing is, your dad asked me not to talk to you for a while—"

"What?" I shake my head. "*Why?* Why would he do that, Quinn? Why is he being so unreasonable?"

"Hey, if I want to be part of your life, then I need to play by his rules. He asked me to give the two of you some time alone, so that's what I'm going to do. I know it sucks, but I think we need to do it his way."

"I hate him for doing this," I say, choking on my anger. "I hate him, Quinn. He doesn't care about what I want. He doesn't care about what's important to me."

"I think he's just upset right now. I'm sure once he's had some time to settle down and work things through, he'll be okay. I really do," he says, recognizing the doubt in my face. "It's going to be okay, Crick."

The hopefulness in his voice is so sincere I almost believe him.

The remainder of our time together slips by like a sandcastle when the tide comes in. I can see it disappearing, feel it being stolen away one second at a time, but there's nothing I can do to stop it. My head tells me I should savor every moment—that I should memorize all of those little things I love about Quinn, the things that won't be clear tomorrow. But my heart is saying something entirely different. It's telling me to hang on and never let go.

"I can't do this, Quinn. I can't say good-bye."

"It's not good-bye. It's *I'll see you soon*."

"No, it's not," I say, turning away from him. "It's more than that, and you know it."

"I know," he says, raising my chin to look at him. His eyes are damp and glistening. "It's a lot more than that. It's *I've had the best summer of my life and I don't want it to end, either*. It's *I think you're amazing and I can't get enough of you*. But more than anything, it's *I love you, Cricket*." Before I can return his sentiment he kisses me, and for a brief moment the world is perfect again.

And then, faster than it materialized, it disappears. "I'll talk to you soon," he says and walks away without another word.

On instinct, I follow after his blurry image, but my feet only manage to carry me so far. It's like my brain knows something my heart hasn't figured out yet.

I don't have a choice. I have to let him go.

TWENTY-SEVEN

According to Dictionary.com, the definition of *alone* is: "Separated from others: isolated."

Never before in the history of the English language has a word's description been more depressing. Or accurate.

From the silent ride home in the backseat to bawling my way through *The Lucky One* last night, I have spent the last thirty hours in virtual solitude. Whatever parental do-good spiel my dad fed Quinn about wanting time alone with me was clearly just a heavy load of Grade A horse crap. He's been locked away in his office since we set foot in the house yesterday. And after ripping Carolyn a new one for involving herself with Rainbow, he took away my phone, iPad, and laptop—effectively squashing any attempt to make contact with the outside world. By six-thirty tonight, it's obvious there's something seriously wrong with me. I used to bask in my cashmere bedding like a cat in the sun; now I find it repulsive. I haven't showered or brushed my teeth since yesterday morning, which probably explains why Mr. Katz won't come near me. If I don't back to my real life soon, I'm going to dial the TLC network myself and beg for an intervention.

I start pounding my feet against the floor while I chuck throw pillow after throw pillow against the wall.

Carolyn's wrinkled face appears in my doorway, interrupting my tirade. "Is everything okay?"

"Yes," I lie. Just like I have the last four hundred times she's asked me. "I'm fine. Just leave me alone."

"Come now." She braves a step inside. Her China blue eyes instantly grow wide when she sees the mess I've made since I've been home. "Oh my," she says, surveying the damage. "You're not okay, are you?"

"What do you think?" I say. "Does this look like the room of someone who's okay?" She ventures farther inside but doesn't answer. "Well, I'm not," I say, when I realize she's not going to respond. "I'm pissed off, Carolyn. I just want to scream, or punch something!" I load my arms with another pillow and throw it, this time at her. It nails her on the leg, but beyond a quick glance downward she hardly flinches.

"Does throwing things make you feel better?" she says, shocking me with her subdued response.

I shake my head.

"That's what I thought." Unflustered by my outburst, she kicks her way through the lace and cashmere landmines that surround her, and pauses at the foot of my bed. "You know what will make you feel better, right?" She spreads her arms out wide as if there are three of me she's trying to accommodate.

I swallow hard as my eyes begin to well with tears. I haven't vol-
untarily hugged Carolyn since the seventh grade.

"It's okay," she says encouragingly.

Apparently all I needed was to hear those two little words,
because I practically leap off the bed and into the safety of her
sturdy embrace. The familiar scent of her rose-scented lotion hits
me, filling me with memories of my childhood. I begin to cry.

"My poor Constance," she says, sniffling back her own, rarely
displayed emotions as she strokes my head. "You've been holding
on to this for too long. It's okay to let it go. Just let it go."

Heeding her instruction, I cry until my throat aches and my
head feels hollow and empty.

"I don't know how you could stand to work for him all these
years," I say. "He's awful. He's a selfish jackass who only cares
about himself."

"No, he's not," she says. Her tone may be soothing, but her
words are still loaded and are beginning to grate on me. "He's a
good man. He's just hurting—"

"*He's* hurting?" I push myself away from her. "He ripped you a
second asshole for honoring the wishes of a dead woman, Carolyn.
How is he the victim?"

"First of all, do not use that language with me. You are a young
lady, Constance, not a sailor. And of course it hurt to be repri-
manded by him, but I betrayed his trust. That's a hard thing for a
man like your father."

"But he screamed at you and said really horrible things."

"Yes, I know. I was there." She takes my hand in hers and gives it a gentle pat. "It's true he said some unkind things, but nothing he said was unexpected. Remember, I've been preparing for that moment for fourteen years."

"So you thought he was wrong then—disrespecting my mother's wishes about Rainbow." I make this a statement and not a question. By the way her narrow lips fold over her teeth to keep from answering, I know I'm right. "Why did you do it then? If you thought he was making the wrong decision?"

"It wasn't about right or wrong, Constance. You were too little to remember, but when she died it nearly destroyed him. He didn't go to work, he didn't eat. He couldn't walk by a picture of her without falling apart. It was all he could do just to get up every day. I had planned to tell him about your mother's request, to share your life with Rainbow, but with his state of mind I didn't think it would be wise, so I did it in secret."

"Knowing he'd react this way when he finally found out."

"Yes," she says, chin cocked. "And I'd do it again. I would have done anything for your mother. She was the most generous, loving woman I have ever known."

"Oh *please*. Spare me the recycled bullshit, Carolyn."

She straightens up. "Excuse me?"

"Come on," I say, dismissing all concern for etiquette or future sailor comparisons. "I've heard every two-minute fundraising blurb about what an incredible person my mother was. How she was generous with her time and talents, how she sought to make the world a better place, blah, blah, blah. Nobody's ever bothered to tell me anything about her. Not the real her!"

"He didn't want me to," she says. She's so quiet I actually squint in the hope of hearing her better.

"What do you mean?"

She stares up at me, her face sagging beneath fourteen years of memories. She looks about a decade older than she did twenty seconds ago. "He told me that my job was to take care of you, and that reminding you of her would only cause you more pain. I wanted to tell you about her, believe me I did, but had I ignored his instructions he would have fired me and hired someone else. A stranger. As much as I hated keeping her from you, I couldn't leave you with a stranger. I didn't have a choice, Constance."

There's a tiny voice inside my head telling me to push her for more reasons to hate my father—the more ammunition, the better. But then there's another voice, this one louder and strangely very similar to Aidan's, that's telling me it's time to stop being angry and to just let it go. I open my mouth, unsure of which little voice will take the prize, when the helpless look on Carolyn's face determines the winner.

"Will you tell me about her now?"

✳ ✳ ✳

Over the next hour I learn that my mother was a horrible cook and that she loved to dance, though she looked like a Labrador on roller skates when she did. Like me, she hated the color orange, and unlike me, thought that buying flowers was a waste of money. She only drank white wine, considered McDonald's french fries one of the five basic food groups, and thought that Aerosmith was the greatest rock band ever. She was kind and funny, ambitious and humble, and generous to a dangerous fault. Like me in a lot of ways—and so very different in others.

"I still don't understand why he didn't want me to know about her," I say. "If he loved her so much, you'd think he would want to talk about her all the time."

"He was coping," she says. "Grief does strange things to people. It was easier for him to push all his feelings away."

"Even feelings about me."

"Well, that's certainly not the case," she says, climbing out of the oversize chair we've been sharing. She gives her blouse a straightening swipe with her hand and faces me with a very serious expression. "He thinks the sun rises and sets in you."

"Yeah, right," I say, and try to keep my eye rolling to a minimum. "So that's why he dragged me away from camp and hasn't spoken to me since?"

She takes a deep breath, her glassy eyes a delicate mixture of frustration and amusement. "I know you're angry, Constance, and I understand why. But you must believe me when I tell you that every decision he's made has been out of love. Just wait," she says, raising her hand to silence me before I have the chance to object. "I'm not telling you what to do," which means she is, "but I want you to keep something in mind. There's no right or wrong way to hurt. Everybody does it their own way. It's how we respond to pain that tells the kind of person we are. And I know that you're a good person, Constance. A *very* good person. Now come here and give me a hug before I leave."

"Where are you going?" I ask, trying to swallow the pearl of wisdom she's just shoved down my throat.

"Bingo at St. Martin's," she says, dropping a parting kiss on my forehead. "Dinner is warming in the oven. I'd really like you to eat something."

"I'll think about it."

"And take a shower," she adds, wrinkling her nose. "That you may *not* think about."

I don't bother to hide my rolling eyes this time.

I wait until I'm sure she's left the house before I venture out of my room. The distinct smell of cheese and garlic hits me right away. Until this moment, my appetite has been virtually nonexistent and easily remedied by a package of Pop-Tarts or a handful of Cheetos. But knowing that one of Carolyn's specialties is just a few rooms away, I'm suddenly starving.

Moving a lot faster than I was ten seconds ago, I pass by the two, never-used guest bedrooms and down the hallway that leads to the formal dining area. I round the mahogany table and half of its fourteen, high-backed chairs, before I enter the kitchen where I come to a screeching halt.

Dad looks up from a tray of piping hot lasagna. His eyes are wide, his mouth stuffed, his fork loaded and ready for another round.

I turn on my heel, prepared to retreat, just as he pulls a fork from the drawer at his side. He slides it in my direction across the granite countertop.

I stare at it, debating whether or not I'm going to stab him with it.

He glances back and forth between me and the fork, before giving the empty bar stool beside him a shove.

I hesitate for a moment, but go over to sit down. I grab my fork and dive in to the opposite end of the tray. We don't speak. We don't look at each other. We just eat.

TWENTY-EIGHT

aturday morning greets me almost as gently as a box of rocks to the head. Almost.

As much as my body appreciates the thirteen hours of carb-induced sleep last night's gorge-fest provided, I still wake up feeling tired and pissed. Not to mention fifty shades of bloated.

I somehow manage to roll my fat ass out of bed and into the kitchen. The lasagna pan Dad and I killed last night is still soaking in the sink. *Ugh.* Just looking at it makes me feel nauseous. I dig a couple of Tums out of the medicine drawer, chew them up quickly, then wash them down with a bottle of Evian, and am just headed back to hibernate in my bedroom when the faint sound of an Eric Clapton song stops me dead in my tracks.

I follow the music through the kitchen and down the hall and come to a stop just outside the media room. Once again, I am shocked to find my dad somewhere other than his office. He's sitting on the sofa, with his attention fixed on the flat screen mounted on the wall in front of him. Thanks to the crack-head architect who designed our house, I can't see what he's watching, so I take the tiniest step inside, careful not to hit that squeaky spot on the floor that will give me away. I drop my bottle, nearly fainting, when my eyes land on the screen.

"Mom."

Before I can process what I'm seeing, Dad whips his head over his shoulder and looks at me. His eyes are red and swollen, his face sagging like his skin grew two sizes overnight.

"She found that dress at a street market outside of Tuscany," he says. His voice sounds scratchy and raw. "She could have had any dress in the world." He turns back to the screen, his voice fading away like the lyrics of a sad country song.

I'd given up asking about a wedding video long ago. You can only hear "it doesn't exist" so many times before you finally call it quits. But as I stand here now, witnessing the full and vibrant life I've only imagined in my head, I feel the need to pinch myself. Too captivated by the image on the screen to know better, I cross the room and sit down on the edge of the cushion beside him.

"She's so beautiful," I say. The way her blonde curls bob like birthday ribbons when she laughs, swaying over the thin, antique lace of her peasant-style dress. Calling her beautiful should be a crime. She's so much more than that.

I watch with bated breath as the images of my youthful father and the woman I know is my mother dance across the screen. Him with his strong chin and proud smile. Her smiling more brightly than the center of the sun. You can actually feel the love between them; it's exactly the way Carolyn described. "Why didn't you show me this before?"

When he doesn't answer, I ask again. "Why didn't you show me this before, Dad?" I turn to look at him and find fresh tears streaming down his face.

"I wanted to," he says. "I did. I wanted you to know everything, I just . . ." His attention shifts from the screen to the floor, "I couldn't."

"I get that it was hard for you," I say, now blurry-eyed myself. "But I had a right to know her, too. Don't you know that?"

"I do," he says, nodding slowly. "You're right. You had every right to know about her. I just couldn't. Seeing her . . . talking about her . . . it just reminded me of how I screwed everything up. How I took her for granted." He pauses to look at me, his swollen eyes locking on mine. "How I took you for granted."

Something deep inside my chest begins to ache, and I'm not sure if I'm going to break or implode. I've always wanted him to own up to what he's done, and to feel like shit for doing it, but now that we're here it doesn't feel right anymore.

"I get it," I blurt out, shocking both of us. "But that still doesn't make it okay. I didn't deserve to be excluded from her life. Just because she wasn't here doesn't mean I didn't want to know her."

He nods his head. "You didn't deserve that. I don't know what else to say to you other than I'm sorry. I am, honey. If I could go back and do things differently I would."

"Well, you can't. The damage has been done and there's no

way to take it back." My words force his expression fade from sad to utterly wounded. "But you can make it better from here on out."

"How?" he says, a twinge of hope coming through his voice. "What do you want me to do?"

"You can start by giving me access to her—to this." I motion to the image in front of us. "I need to know who she was even if it's hard for you. She's part of what makes me who I am."

"Okay," he says with a slow nod.

"And I need you to get over the whole Rainbow thing. I know you don't like her, but she was a big part of Mom's life and I think she might be a big part of mine, too." This obviously catches him by surprise and his eyes grow wide. "I haven't figured out exactly what kind of relationship I'm going to have with her," I say. "But I will have one. And I'm also going back to work there next summer."

"You want to go back?"

"Yes. You might not believe it, but I'm now officially the best kid in the world because of that place."

His brows arch high into his forehead and he lets out a short laugh, offering a glimpse of his friendlier side.

"Okay, maybe not the *best* kid in the world, but I'm definitely a lot better than I was. I get that you were trying to protect me by insulating me in a world you had control over, but that doesn't work for me—not anymore. You can't keep me all bottled up anymore."

"Wow," he says, taking in my demands with a quick shake of his head. "You weren't kidding about changing—"

"And then there's Quinn," I say, saving the most important condition for last. "You need to be okay with him, too."

"No," he says. "That's one I can't budge on. He's a bad influence, Cricket. There's no telling what kind of trouble a boy like that will get you into."

I can't help but laugh. "You're kidding, right?"

He crosses his arms over his chest.

"Dad, I know you can't see it yet, but Quinn is probably the best influence I've ever had in my life. Once you get to know him, you'll see it, too." He opens his mouth like he's going to argue, so I quickly cut him off before he has the chance. "It's non-negotiable," I say with more conviction than I've ever said anything before. "Quinn's part of my life now. You accept him or you lose me. That's all there is to it."

Looking like he's just been kissed by a fastball, he settles back into the cushions and takes a deep breath. It's the kind of breath you see men in movies take before they agree to buy their kid a car even though their grades are in the toilet. The kind of breath that says I'm going to trust you, so please don't let me down. "Did you know your mother was prelaw when we first started dating?" he asks.

I shake my head. "I had no idea."

"Well, she was." There's a hint of a smile breaking through his tired face. It looks good on him. "And in all the years we were together, I never won an argument. You sounded exactly like her just then."

I feel my heart swell beneath my chest and I swallow hard. "Okay," he says, raising his palms in surrender. "I'll give the boy a chance. Is there anything else?"

"Actually, yes. There is *one* more thing. . . ."

TWENTY-NINE

"A re you sure we're going the right way?" From her shotgun position, Carolyn leans forward and gives the GPS a smack. "Maybe this thing is broken—"

"Stop!" I say, swatting at her. "We're going the right way."

"Are you certain?" She drops her head slightly and peers through the windshield into dusky night. "You were riding in the backseat the last time you came here. And it was daylight."

"I'm positive," I say, casting a subtle glance at the map illuminating from the dashboard. "At least I think I am."

According to my sometimes-accurate navigation system, we should be coming up on the Camp I Can turnoff any minute now. Although with the way my nerves are bouncing around, it wouldn't surprise me if I missed it thirty miles ago.

"Maybe your father was right," she says. "If we had just let Sean drive us, we wouldn't have to worry about any of this."

"*God*, we're going the right way," I say again. My wingman's dwindling confidence is starting to get annoying. "It should be around one of these corners."

Her heavy sigh only adds to my own uncertainty. Because it

took a few hours to convince Dad to let me and my sixty-year-old chaperone take this battle-of-the-bands road trip, we got out of the house later than I would have liked. And despite the extra hours of daylight a Midwestern summer provides, it's still tricky navigating through all the shadows and turns that make up this highway.

"Oh, there it is!" I whip my arm across Carolyn's chest and point to the sign that says, CAMP I CAN, 1 MILE. The first time I saw that sign it made my stomach turn. Tonight it just makes me giggle.

We pull off the highway and onto the dirt road that leads to camp. Stupid as it sounds, I roll down my window and inhale the familiar air.

"Slow down," Carolyn says. "Are you trying to kill us?"

I glance down at the speedometer and cringe. "Sorry," I say, easing up on the pedal a smidge. "But we're already late, and I'm *dying* to get there."

"To see the boy," she says.

I feel my cheeks flush. "Among other things . . ."

Though I've only traveled this road four times before (three sober), I know at exactly what point the mess hall will come into view; just around this bend. . . . My hands tighten on the wheel, and I exhale a nervous breath.

"Anticipation is good for the soul," Carolyn says, patting my leg.

"Then my soul must be pretty freaking happy right now."

We make the final turn and, as expected, the rickety building comes into view. "There it is," I say, a smile erupting across my face.

"Oh my. That's not hard to miss, is it?"

Her tone suggests that her first impression isn't too different than mine was. But that's the beauty of first impressions—before you know it they're forgotten.

"Wait until you see the inside," I say. "We were designing different sets for every act. We made this huge Eiffel Tower for the full group routine, and Colin had this whole underground, industrial thing for his. They were going to install colored lights if they could find any. I wonder if they did," I say, interrupting my own train of thought.

"Oh, Constance, she would have been very proud of you," Carolyn says, chuckling at my enthusiasm.

I glance over at her. "Who?"

"Your mother."

Emotions prick at my eyes, forcing me to swallow hard.

"It's okay," she says, patting my leg. "Your mother was sensitive, too."

"She was?"

"Mmm-hmm. It's a gift you know. Not everyone has that kind of connection to things . . . and people." She motions to the parking area that comes into view in front of us and I smile. There are at least a dozen cars in the lot, which means all the parents showed up as hoped. Awesome.

Sniffling back my emotions, I pull up beside the beater camp pickup, and before I even cut the engine I hear the all-too familiar lyrics of "Radioactive" thumping from inside the building.

"We gotta hurry," I say. "Colin's group is on right now, and I'm not sure what order they're going in."

"Go ahead," she says, fumbling with her seat belt. "I'll catch up with you."

I hesitate for a moment, but the sound of applause puts me back in motion.

"I'll see you inside," I call over my shoulder, already halfway across the lot. I clear the weathered steps two at a time, round the rickety porch, and blow straight through the front doors. Besides a strand of white Christmas lights lining the perimeter of the stage, the room is dark. And other than the whispers of audience members, completely quiet as well.

Crap. I've missed Colin's performance.

"You're here!"

I turn over my shoulder and find Rainbow standing just a few feet away. Illuminated only by the last remnants of daylight seeping in through the open door behind me, she looks paler than ever. And completely surprised.

"I'm so glad you made it," she says. "I can't believe he let you come."

"That makes two of us," I say. Rainbow leans forward and pulls me in for a hug. It's a little awkward, but not completely horrible. "So what'd we miss?"

"We?"

"Carolyn came with me. She's still fighting with her seat belt in the parking lot."

"Carolyn's here? That's . . . wow," she says. It takes her a moment to regain what little composure she had. "Okay," she clears her throat. "So, what'd you miss? Uh, nothing actually." She nods toward a flashing red light in the corner. "We've been recording the entire thing . . . for you, that is. We started with the group performance, and Fantine's and Colin's groups just finished. . . ."

"Aw, man. I wanted to see everybody's."

"I'm sorry. But you know how it goes around here. If we don't stay on schedule the whole thing gets thrown off."

"Right," I say. Once a schedule Nazi . . .

"They all went beautifully, though," she adds. "Especially the group performance. Fantine filled in as Madonna and *really* worked that cone bra."

I can't help but laugh. Of course she did.

"So Quinn's up next?" I ask hopefully.

She shakes her head, but any verbal response she'd planned to give me is interrupted when the boy in question's soothing voice interrupts her over the aging PA system.

"Ladies and gentlemen," he says. "Please welcome to the stage, Team Daniel-san performing, 'Hollaback Girl.'"

"They're still doing our act?" I say, my eyes growing wide as the stage lights flicker on in a sea of color. I turn my attention back to

Rainbow. "Who's filling in for me?"

"See for yourself!" she says, pointing to the stage as the audience begins to cheer.

I reface the front of the room and my jaw instantly drops like it's loaded with concrete.

Meredith is still sporting a cheerleader uniform as originally planned, but it's Claire who has taken a major detour with her choice of costume. Shimmery silver leggings are stretched tight across every inch of her ample bottom half, while her top is poured into a white sports bra that could probably double as a hammock at this point. Beneath the colorful lights, the rolls of belly fat sandwiched between the two garments gleam like dough waiting for the oven, but based on the size of Claire's smile, she doesn't care. Good-bye, chunky cheerleader, hello, plus-sized Stefani.

"Holy shit," I sputter, fanning my hands over my eyes.

"Isn't it that something?" Rainbow says, smiling.

"Oh, it's something all right."

The drumbeat moves quickly, and much to my surprise so do both of them. Just as we'd rehearsed, Meredith kicks off the routine by showing off her upper body strength. She's hand-standing her way across the stage, while Claire plods along beside her, punching her fist through the air as she spouts off the opening monologue like a rapper. Much to my surprise, she's on top of the lyrics, and is about to deliver the last lines before the actual melody picks up, when she suddenly stops in her tracks. Eyes squinted beneath the brim of her black beanie, she clomps to the edge of the stage.

"Cricket!" she says into the microphone. "Is that you?"

My cheeks flood with embarrassment, as every audience member turns their head in my direction. I nod quickly, encouraging her to carry on with a wave of my hand.

"You came back!" she says, pointing at me. "Meredith, look. Cricket came back!"

Meredith drops to the ground, and from the push-up position smiles broadly in my direction. "Hiiiiii, Cricket! Hoooooow are youuuu?"

"I'm fine!" I shout over an eruption of laughter from the audience. "I'll talk to you later. But now you need to keep going!"

"What?" Claire yells.

"Finish the song!"

"Oh right," Claire says, nodding. "We need to finish."

"Riiiiight," says Meredith.

"Do you want to sing with us?" Claire says.

I shake my head. "No. You're doing great!"

It takes a moment, but after a few stutters and stumbles the girls manage to get relatively back on track with the music, and that's when I begin to laugh.

"They're pretty amazing, aren't they?" Rainbow says, leaning against me.

I nod. "They are."

As anticipated, the word *bananas* poses a problem for Claire, and the routine has more than a few hiccups including one collision in front of the yellow convertible prop, but no one seems to notice. In the end, it's as tragic as it is funny, but it's still a home run and I'm like a proud parent watching from the bleachers.

"That was so awesome," I say, swiping tears from my eyes. "They did such a good job." I look to Rainbow expecting to find her nodding along in agreement, but she's no longer beside me. I turn over my opposite shoulder and through the dim light find her near the doorway with Carolyn. They're tittering like school girls on the playground. A smile pushes its way across my face. They've got a lot to talk about.

"Hey, sexy," a familiar voice says against my ear. I turn over my opposite shoulder and find Fantine standing right beside me, still wearing the tongue-depressor bra.

"Me, how about you?" I say, pulling her in for a tight hug, which isn't easy given her pointy boobs. "You are so rocking that bra, girl!"

She steps away from me, grinning. "I do what I can," she says. "So how in the hell did you manage to get back here? I heard your dad was pretty pissed the other day."

"Oh, he was. But we've been talking a lot and . . . I don't know, I guess we've reached an understanding for how things are going to work from now on."

"Well, that's good," she says. "And please tell me this under-standing includes you hanging out with Mr. Efron."

"It does."

"Thank you, Jesus," she says with a sigh. "He's been moping around here like a lost puppy ever since you left. I was starting to think he needed an intervention or something."

"Really?"

She nods. "Of course his mood changed when he heard Claire call you out onstage."

"Really?" I ask again.

"Yep. He went from Mr. Mopey, *how am I going to do this routine?*, to Mr. Nervous Jitters in about two seconds."

"Why would Quinn be nervous? He's been practicing for two weeks."

A wave of gasps suddenly fills the mess hall as the lights are cut, rendering the room completely dark.

"Just wait," she says.

"And now for a very special final performance. . . ." The arrival of Quinn's voice generates a round of applause and whistles, but the room stays dark. My heart starts beating a little faster. "Team Oven Mitt would like to dedicate this song to someone who was very special to everyone at camp this summer—especially me. Cricket was the driving force of this entire production and should be recognized for all of her hard work." He pauses briefly while the crowd can claps. "So Miss Montgomery," he says, "this one's for you."

His tender words tug on my heart, as I join the rest of the

crowd in waiting for something, anything, to happen.

"What's just for me?" I ask Fantine anxiously. "What's he going to do?"

"Just shut up and watch."

A moment passes before a narrow beam of white light cascades across center stage and a six-foot silhouette emerges from behind the curtain. The butterflies in my stomach immediately flutter to life.

Beyond restless, the crowd begins to yelp and holler as Quinn slowly makes his way across the stage. Just before he reaches the tiny circle of light, drum-thumping music erupts through the outdated sound system and the rest of the stage explodes in a thousand watts of color, revealing Quinn and his three assigned campers, Chase, Trevor, and James. They're each holding a basketball and wearing a red-and-white basketball uniform with the word WILDCATS printed on the front.

"No way," I say, shaking my head in disbelief.

I'm not sure which is to blame, the workout clothes or the cocky smirk he's wearing, but one of them sends a flush of goose bumps across my skin. I make a move for the nearest chair, stopping short when Quinn's gleaming blue gaze locks in on me. At first I think it's impossible for him to see me considering the amount of wattage shining in his face, but as his mouth turns up into that lopsided grin I love so much, I know I've been made. I smile back at him before collapsing into the chair.

"Oh boy," I say to myself. Dad may have been right after all. There's no telling what kind of trouble this guy could get me in to.

Zac Efron, eat your heart out.

Author's
NOTE

I t would be easy to assume that *Summer on the Short Bus* was inspired by my special needs daughter, but it wasn't—not really. It's true that elements of her quirky nature were integrated into some of the characters, but the real inspiration for this book had more to do with my own journey in getting to know her, understanding her differences, and above all, determining how I was going to build an authentic relationship with her while remaining true to my *own* quirky nature.

As someone whose diet consists heavily of sarcasm and irreverence, it was important for me to bring those elements to this story in a genuine way. There is nothing politically correct about *Summer on the Short Bus*, nor is there an intentional message of inclusion in these pages. This story is merely a stage for an honest character to evolve realistically (no matter how ugly), something we don't see enough of these days.

I like to quote MTV's *The Real World* opening monologue when describing this book to people. *Summer on the Short Bus* is "What happens when people stop being polite and start getting real." And in a world where every kid earns a trophy at the end of the season, I think a little *real* is long overdue.

—*Bethany Crandell*

ACKNOWLEDGMENTS

Endless thanks to . . .

Terry, Gracie, and Becca. Your sacrifices of my time and attention (and well-balanced meals) allowed this dream to become a reality.

My parents. You always encouraged me to be myself, no matter the repercussions. And my sisters, Angie and Lori. You've been by my side every step of this journey. We may be down a man, but our army is still strong.

Rachael Dugas for believing in me and placating the voices with a laugh.

Marlo Scrimizzi. Your counsel, wisdom, and enthusiasm for this book cannot be measured. I am a better writer because of you—and your perfectly timed chocolates. And to the entire Running Press family for taking a chance on this unique story and allowing my voice to have a home.

My crit partner and soul-sister, Anita Howard. What can I say . . . this birdbath was built for two.

My A-Team. Each of you makes me a better friend. And you

laugh at my jokes—wow.

Jill Badonsky. You convinced me that I had a story to tell and that crappy first drafts are part of the process.

My beloved Goat Posse. If not for you, I'd have pulled out all of my hair by now. (And we all know that's no easy feat.)

The YA Valentines. This has been an incredible debut year. Your support of me, and each other, is astounding.

Laura Walker and Heather Hernandez for braving the Peggy Flemming waters and encouraging me to keep swimming no matter how long it took. And Andrea Riklin, you should charge me for cut, color, *and* therapy.

The girls on the fourth floor. On our own, we're just quirky individuals, but together we are a beautiful, dysfunctional mess— with very nice handbags.

Nicole Resciniti and Robyn Russell for the continued applause, even after the no.

My WrAHM sisters. Your support, banter, and motivational images saved me on more than one occasion. The talented writers at OneFour KidLit, and on Query Tracker and Twitter. This experience has been so much better because I got to share it with all of you.

There are so many more, but since the band has started to play, I'll conclude with the most important: my Heavenly Father. Maybe one day I will learn that your timing is better than mine. Until then, your grace is enough.

JUV
FIC
CRANDELL

Crandell, Bethany,
 author.

Summer on the short
 bus.

$9.95   05/06/2014

DATE			

DAMAGED

Yellow stains + water
damage on middle
pages of book.
08/23/18 Ⓜ

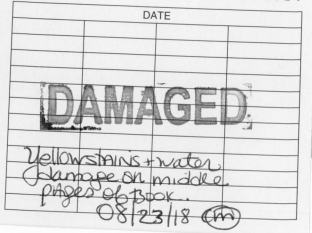

HILLSIDE PUBLIC LIBRARY
155 LAKEVILLE RD
NEW HYDE PARK NY 11040

BAKER & TAYLOR